BLAZER: LOADED

G.C. HARMON

ROUGH EDGES PRESS

ROUGH EDGES PRESS

Paperback Edition
Copyright © 2022 (As Revised) G.C. Harmon

Published in the United States by Wolfpack Publishing, Las Vegas

Rough Edges Press
An Imprint of Wolfpack Publishing
5130 S. Fort Apache Rd. 215-380
Las Vegas, NV 89148

roughedgespress.com

Paperback ISBN: 978-1-68549-005-8
eBook ISBN: 978-1-68549-004-1

BLAZER: LOADED

INTRODUCTION

I started writing this story in 2010 when California first tried to legalize recreational marijuana. Now that it has been legalized, I foresee problems, and I had to speak up.

Much of this story comes from personal experience, which I think is different than most people's. We've been led to believe that pot smokers are those harmless lovable losers we see in the movies. We've rationalized this drug to the point where society believes *it's no big deal*. I've seen another side. A large percentage of marijuana smokers experience forms of psychosis. I've seen that psychosis, along with the lives wasted. In my day job, I've had my life threatened by those that smoke the stuff, simply because I ask them to follow the rules. The psychotic behavior, the wasted potential of one's life, the gateway effect, they're all real. I've seen them firsthand. But those who support marijuana use don't want you to know about it. They don't want you to know the problems that have arisen from other states that have legalized. But those problems are coming. This book is a warning. In a sick irony, I finished writing this story at *4:20* in the afternoon—if you don't understand the reference, you should.

DEDICATION

This book is for all the victims of marijuana use.
I was one.

CHAPTER 1

The greenery of Golden Gate Park gave the area a unique beauty, but as one looked up at the blue morning sky and then moved their gaze down to the trees, that beauty ended at eye level. Sheltered by the trees of the east end of the Golden Gate Park Panhandle was a segment of humanity that seemed completely lost. This was Haight Ashbury, a district of San Francisco with a history steeped in music and a version of peace and love. It was a decadence that made its mark in the history books. Decadence of a new kind lay like a diverse quilt over the neighborhood now. The history of the Haight was enough to still draw tourists, but those tourists had to navigate streets lined with society's outcasts.

Walking among them was a San Francisco cop, a very special cop. Steve Blazer was one of the more dedicated officers of the SFPD. When he first joined the department, he was already a veteran of the war on terror, serving a tour with Special Forces first in Afghanistan, and then a year later was part of the force that invaded Iraq. On SFPD, he accumulated a long arrest record while in uniform, especially when it came to drug arrests. This led to special training with the SWAT team, as well as a year on the Vice Squad. While doing a tour as a Homicide Inspector, he was tapped for a special detail. He was put in charge of assembling a crack squad of Inspectors, ironically to be named simply "Special Forces."

But after a rough start, that squad was disbanded before it could create any more controversy. Knowing this city the way he did, Steve knew there would be a need to bring the team together again. In fact, he had designs along that line now.

He had come to the Haight on a specific mission, and it had to do with the lost segment of humanity surrounding him. His trained eye searched his surroundings. He picked out a pair of transients camped out on the sidewalk, wrapped in dirty blankets, their prone forms stretched out across the walkway, so they impeded travel. Another grungy looking man sat on a patch of grass across the street, openly drinking from a can of beer, even at nine a.m. The can was covered by a wrinkled paper bag, but Steve knew what was in that bag. If the beverage was non-alcoholic, why hide it in the bag? Steve paused as he watched another unkempt man amble across the street in his direction. The man passed him and stepped up to a nearby building. He paused at a corner of one shop, politely away from the door to the business. He seemed to be leaning against the wall, but Steve soon saw liquid seeping around the man's dirty shoes—he was urinating there.

Steve's traveling companion saw this too, and she recoiled in disgust. He looked at her and could only offer a smile that conveyed sympathy for the revolting act they were witnessing. The woman, Officer Susan Wolf, was five foot eight, and had long blonde hair that she wore down today while wearing plain clothes, simple jeans and a T-shirt. Steve had been dating her for just a couple months, but he was feeling an intense connection to her. Steve himself was six foot two and dressed similarly, in jeans and a green polo shirt. This was high fashion compared to the rags worn by those clustered in this area. Both cops wore jackets that hid their police issue sidearms, as well as protected them from a cool breeze off the ocean. It was now late December; Christmas was just a memory of twenty-four hours ago. Some local shops still displayed a few remaining decorations, but for most, it was as if they were eager to put the holiday behind them, sweep it back into the closet for the year, out of sight, out of mind. For the week between Christmas and New Year's, it was time to get back to work.

"It makes you wonder how far mankind has to sink before we can police ourselves," Steve smiled at Suzy.

"Is this what we're looking for?" she asked.

"There," Steve said, pointing at a doorway at the end of the block, the south-west corner of the intersection of Oak and Baker Streets. They walked in a little closer, and found a sign painted on the glass door: "Green Resolve." A man in a dingy jacket walked out that door carrying a crumpled paper bag. He crossed the street to the two guys laying on the grass. He knelt down next to them, and the three of them hungrily attacked the paper bag. In moments, all three were lighting hand-rolled cigarettes. The breeze blew tendrils of smoke in their directions and Suzy recoiled at the smell. They weren't smoking tobacco.

Steve gestured at the door. "This right here is a Cannabis dispensary. Hippie history aside, this area was once a nice neighborhood. This place opened just two months ago. Like every other pot dispensary in this city, the neighborhood went off a cliff as soon as it opened. These places are supposed to be where people can get 'medicinal marijuana'. But true to form, they attract every doper who can lie to a doctor. In the last month, PD has received over a hundred nuisance complaints for the very thing we're seeing. Transients everywhere, panhandling, public intoxication, public urination. For some reason, unlike other dispensaries, this place does not have a security guard to curtail most of this misdemeanor behavior. So, we have dopers taking advantage of a law that was misguided to begin with."

"You don't believe in medical marijuana?"

"I think it's a myth. Sure, there's a few worst-case scenarios, where maybe a patient dying of cancer can't keep meds down and somehow marijuana settles an upset stomach. Even in those cases, weed does more damage than anyone is willing to admit. Years ago, Californians voted to legalize marijuana for medicinal use. Stoners now had a way to get high legally and they hijacked the whole medicinal marijuana phenomenon. For a while, anyone could bribe a doctor and say—," he took on a mocking tone, "Oh, I have a bad back. Oh, I get headaches." The most common excuse is a very generic 'chronic pain.' The doctor gives them a recommendation, but in their mind, it's a prescription. That means, in their mind, marijuana is no longer a controlled narcotic. It's medicine. And medicine is supposed to be good for you."

"Lots of people get headaches," Suzy suggested.

"Weed is not supposed to be your first line of defense against a minor throb. How many pot dispensaries do we have in this city? Do that many people actually get those severe headaches? Even in a city this size, you would think maybe a handful of dispensaries, ten, twelve. We have over a hundred in San Francisco. Are there really that many sick people to cater to?

"Society has been moving toward rationalizing marijuana use for a long time. It's just one joint, it's no big deal. I saw this all the time when I was in uniform. I made a lot of DUI stops where the driver hadn't been drinking, he'd been *smoking*. I saw the accidents too. But I could see society moving toward excusing marijuana use. District Attorneys stopped prosecuting pot cases. Knowing this, I still pushed through marijuana DUI cases, because I see how dangerous those kinds of DUIs are. I wanted the DAs to see that too, for all the good it did." He blew out a sigh. "And now California has legalized marijuana for personal use."

Suzy nodded. "Everyone's scrambling to create a system of regulations for when the law goes into effect on January 1st."

"I guarantee you, Suzy, those DUIs, and DUI accidents will go up, we'll see a spike in all that." He gestured around him. "We'll see a lot more of this."

"Keep in mind, Steve," Suzy said, "I do agree with you. But let me play devil's advocate for a minute. Activists are using this issue to suggest it will help California with its financial crisis. Everyone says that if you can tax it and regulate it, you can generate millions of dollars. They say that marijuana taxes can rescue the state from its perpetual recession."

Steve shook his head and chuckled. "First of all, when has government done something like this where it has worked? Government can't control marijuana for the purposes of eradication, how are they going to control it for the purposes of taxation? How many people have you seen during the course of doing this job that have their own plants? Is the government going to now forbid that so the pot shops can make money for them? Second, all that will do is create more welfare cases that use the stuff. Usage will spike. People's attitude about it will be, look, it's legal, that means it's not harmful. Crimes related to usage will spike, no one is making that connection. Burglaries, robberies, DUIs, all will spike. As for the pushers and drug rings and cartels out there, don't you think they're going to try to find a way around the laws to make their money? Are they going to let the government take their market away? It will create a whole new black market for marijuana that will compete with the government and those of us who fight to take dope off the street will be right back where we started. But now, as cops, we'll be protecting the 'legal drug dealers' against the black-market street punks. That doesn't sit right with me."

"OK, next talking point," Suzy said, "Everyone says that pot is harmless, it's natural, it's pure and comes from the earth."

"There are a lot of things in nature that can kill you. Sure, weed is just another plant—until you light it on fire and release all those toxins into your body. And at that point, we both know the effects. Short term, it affects the brain, lowers inhibitions, etc. Long term it affects your memory, kills off the brain cells, stunts mental growth in teens, not to mention the damage to your lungs after smoking for so long. How many times have cops encountered someone going through some kind of psychosis brought on by inhaling the smoke of a simple plant?"

Suzy was getting into her devil's advocate role. "What about alcohol or tobacco? Those have been proven to be harmful, and they're still legal. They even tried prohibition of alcohol, remember?"

Steve smiled at this. "Not a lot of people know these statistics. Yeah, there was a rise of crime and speakeasies, it gave birth to Al Capone and organized crime. But people don't realize that alcohol consumption actually went *down* during Prohibition. The two situations don't really compare. Alcohol and tobacco are both heavily regulated, at least they are supposed to be. Analysts can't yet figure out how to regulate marijuana. Despite the efforts of drug crusaders like myself, weed is still extremely easy to find. It's easy for a kid to get his hands on some weed."

"Isn't that evidence that the drug war is lost?"

Her question hit a nerve. Steve had been almost giddy as he made his arguments. Now his face darkened. "That is something I can never accept. The drug war is not lost—it was never really fought. Yeah, this country paid it some lip service back in the 80s and 90s. I spent a lot of time with Army Special Forces doing anti-drug operations in South America, and some of that spilled over into the streets of Miami when I lived there. But gradually the druggies pushed back. They used the law against law enforcement. How many drug cases have you seen that were air-tight get thrown out on a technicality that may or may not have been legit? Or they get thrown out because of lies and spun facts? That's how cops get disillusioned, and that's how they get susceptible to bribes. Meanwhile, every movie out there portrays weed smokers as stupid, funny and harmless. Can you say social engineering? Gradually, the public has had their attitude adjusted to now accept marijuana as harmless. What's next? Where does society draw the line as to what is acceptable?" He paused, and the dark look on his face became a thousand-yard stare. "There's a code that I long ago accepted in my career that holds true for everything I do as a cop. The battle between good and evil may seem like a losing battle, but it's a battle that must be fought, or civilized society is lost."

Suzy thought for a moment. To any of the stoners

or brain-dead people around them, his words would have sounded stupid and preachy. But she could see that he truly believed them. She knew him well, had seen him in action, and she knew a simple statement like that was what drove him. Deep down, she felt the same, even if in a more distant way.

She hated to dash the solemn moment. "Even with all that, Steve, it's still a personal choice. Each of them made the choice to do drugs."

"That's why I don't have any sympathy when someone ends up in my handcuffs. But it's not about them. It always affects someone else. Take a look around you, Suzy. Does this look like our society is heading in the right direction? Every one of these people started out differently than this. No matter what environment you grew up in, you had a chance to make the right choice and make something of your life. To reduce it to terms for this situation here, you're offered a choice, to smoke weed or to not. They made their choice. But as cops, we *can* affect it. If I can take some dope off the street, then the pusher that would have had that dope will not have it to offer some poor unsuspecting kid tonight, and that kid will not be presented with that choice, to smoke or not to smoke. He gets another day without drugs screwing him up to seek his own positive way through life."

They were standing near the doorway. While animated, their conversation had quieted down. Steve saw a customer come out of the Cannabis Club. He was tall, black but with light skin, and he wore a tank top, even in the cool morning, that showed off a ripped muscular physique, studded with a handful of tattoos. Steve eyed the man as he turned away from the plainclothes cops and walked around the side of the building.

"Take this guy, for instance," he said. She'd gotten

a brief look at him. Steve grabbed her hand and led her to the corner. Their subject had turned south on Baker Street, and Steve stopped at the intersection, watching the guy as he walked away. "This guy is built like a tank, does he look like needs medical marijuana—" he cut off as the man stopped, just behind the building, where a narrow alley opened. It was too narrow for a vehicle to travel, but it made a good hiding place. They watched two teenage boys step out of the alley. The black man stopped just within sight and handed over the bag, and Steve saw one of the boys hand over a small handful of cash. The black man took it and hurried on his way.

"Just one of many crimes associated with legalization of marijuana, people abusing their privileges," Steve said. "I think we should talk to these kids."

Intent on the transaction, they did not see another young man wearing a dark hooded sweatshirt hurry across the street toward them. He approached from their left and suddenly loomed in front of them. He was short and scrawny, wearing grungy dark pants and a dirty hoodie, not pulled tight but still mostly shielding his face.

Steve stopped short, seeing the gun in the man's hand. It was a snub-nose .38 revolver, but it was still a deadly piece, and it was pointed right at him. "Give me your money, now!" the man croaked.

Everyone froze.

An eternal second later, with the gun still trained loosely on his center mass, Steve turned to Suzy. "See, this is what I'm talking about. This guy is just a stoner. He doesn't have any obvious health conditions that would *entitle* him to be hanging out near a pot shop. He just wants to get high and do it on my dime."

"He's still got the gun," Suzy said, nerves evident in her voice more so than Steve's.

"Nah, he's shaking, he's all over the place." Steve began moving his hands about as he spoke. "He's never going to hit anything. Drugs will do that to you."

The young man seemed agitated that his robbery was not going well. He had the gun, why would these people not do what he demanded? "I said give me your money. Now!"

Steve turned back to him, offered an annoyed shrug. "Shut up, man, I'm making a point here. What do you want with my money anyway? You're just going to score weed, right?"

"I got a gun, man!"

"You really don't know how to use that thing, do you?" Steve said. "Look, you're so scared, you pissed yourself."

Everything Steve had said and done in the last thirty seconds was distraction, a way to divide and misguide the robber's attention while he waited for his opening. It came when the man's wild eyes darted for one instant away from his targets. Steve's waving hands came together in a steel grip around the robber's gun hand. He twisted them just right until the robber was staring into the barrel of his own gun.

Steve held the man's arm for a moment and pulled him closer. He had total control of the gun—it was pointed at the user, but the user's hand was twisted around to where he could not easily pull the trigger. Steve let his eyes go wild for just an instant. "You want to pull the trigger now?"

The robber could only let out a terrified squeal.

"Brace yourself," Steve said, "this is going to hurt."

He stepped back and turned, pulling the robber into a throw, while still maintaining his grip on the gun and hand. With legs flailing, the robber went to the ground, but his arm stayed vertical, hand held in Steve's grip. Steve used the arm to position the suspect on his belly. He gently pulled the gun from the man's grip and handed it to Suzy. In a series of smooth motions, coming from years of practice, Steve pulled his cuffs from a back pocket, and quickly subdued the suspect. "By the way," he told his suspect, "I should let you know, I'm a cop." His badge was on a chain around his neck, and he pulled it out of his shirt. "Just to get a few bucks for some dope, you committed a felony robbery, and on two police officers. Was it worth it?"

Steve glanced up at Suzy. She had taken a single step back and was now on her cell phone, calling for a patrol unit.

Steve then noticed a new danger approaching. Some of the people that he'd been watching for the last few minutes had seen him take the robber to the ground. They were now emerging from the trees of the panhandle, like zombies from the mist. They crossed the street, coming closer. One man, white and about thirty with long unkempt hair, got brave and stepped forward. "What are you doing to my friend, man?"

"Police, sir, please stay back. Your friend is under arrest."

"Why can't you cops quit hassling innocent people?" The long-hair took another step forward. "You're checking out the pot shop, ain't you? The stuff's legal now. Where were you cops when my stash got stolen out of my car yesterday?"

You're proving my point, Steve thought. "Sir, I'll ask you again to step back."

"You wouldn't be so tough with someone my size," the long-hair said. He spat on the ground. "Let's see you take me down."

Steve rose to his full height, bringing him practically eye-to-eye with the man—he was an inch taller. The man had reached the curb and was now just eight feet away.

Suzy stepped up between Steve and the long-hair. "Police business!" She did not yell but said it forcefully enough that anyone with a conscience would have thought twice about disobeying. "Back away!"

Not this guy. He looked down at her with a smirk that seemed to say, do you really think *you* are going to stop me?

Suzy's right hand flashed upward. She clasped an ASP, a collapsible baton. The flick of her arm extended the baton with a loud clacking noise. It was one final gesture of intimidation for the angry druggie, one last chance for him to think twice about taking on the Police.

He made his choice quickly and lunged at her.

Suzy quickly brought the baton down, grasping it across her body with the handle in her right hand. That side lashed out, jabbing the man sharply in the sternum. It stopped his charge, but he raised his arms to grab such a close-up target. Suzy stepped quickly to her left, and she brought the baton down in a swing across her body. The blow caught the long-hair behind his knee. He cried out as his legs buckled, and he went to the pavement. Suzy kicked at him, catching him in the shoulder and knocking him onto his side. She brought the baton back, ready for a vicious swing, but she checked herself, poised over him. "You want some more?" she shouted. "Stay down!"

The long-hair stayed down.

"Nice moves," Steve commented from the sidewalk. Both he and Suzy scanned the sidewalk for anyone else wanting to interfere with their arrest.

A blast of siren cut into the confrontation. The approaching crowd stopped and started to back away. A black and white Ford Crown Victoria patrol unit eased onto the scene, driving slowly into the crowd to entice them to back away. Steve made sure his badge was visible as two uniformed officers stepped out. Steve recognized the senior officer, a man he'd worked and trained with. "Officer Norris, this one is in custody for 211 with a gun. Let's get him in the cage. I'm still considering assault charges on this one."

Norris and his partner handled the suspect, cuffing him and easing him into the back seat of their car. Steve conducted a quick search on the long hair and found a small baggie of marijuana on the subject. He quickly opened the baggie and dumped the contents into the gutter. He waited for the long hair to voice an objection, but none was forthcoming. Steve didn't even think the guy registered his stash being found.

Norris returned. "What about this guy?"

Steve shrugged. "Cite and release, 242," giving the penal code for the crime of battery. "He'll probably never see court."

Norris glanced over as a second unit pulled up behind his. He knelt over the long hair. "Come on, partner, you awake? Let's go have a chat." The man sat up on his own, and Norris helped him up.

Suzy handed off the gun to Norris to log as evidence, then turned to Blazer. "Are we done here?"

"Not a chance," Steve said. He glanced at the gathering dope heads looking on at the action, then back to the door of the cannabis dispensary. "I'm just getting started."

CHAPTER 2

Kevin Donner and his friend Randy Shepherd walked north on Baker Street, then Randy led them across to a small alley. As they entered, Kevin got a glimpse of a muscular black man approaching from the corner. He entered the alley and contacted Randy. "I got your text kid. Cookie Crush, two buds. Green for the green."

"Got you covered, Lynell." Randy handed over a bill, and the black man handed over the bag. "I'll text if I need something else."

Lynell gave him a condescending look. "Yeah." He started to step away, but the boys ran past him, leaving the alley.

They were completely unaware of the commotion that happened outside the dispensary just moments later.

They jogged the first block, just to get away from any prying eyes that might connect two teenage guys to the neighborhood around a pot shop. They now walked the neighborhood at a quick march. Kevin felt a little paranoid. Like his buddy, he was only seventeen, and the last thing he wanted was to get caught holding weed. He refused to acknowledge that those paranoid feelings might be the last shreds of his conscience. Randy did not seem to have such hang-ups.

"Who was that guy, anyway?" Kevin asked. This was the first time he'd bought from the guy, but Randy knew him.

"He's my dad's friend's brother, something like that. I smoked with him a few months ago when we were over for dinner. The guy's got a doctor's note. He says it was so easy to get one. Somebody hooked him up with a doctor who took bribes. Slip him a hundred bucks and the doc writes you a scrip for medical cannabis. He told me the doc got busted, but he found a couple other doctors, and he sends them business. One of his doc friends he says is eager to prescribe the stuff. As soon as I turn eighteen, I'm paying him a visit."

"You could just get a fake ID."

Randy stopped, a grin spreading across his face. "Dude, that's freaking brilliant. I knew there was a reason I kept you around. Anyway, Lynell set up his own side business. You place your order, he'll hit up a dispensary and get it for you. At a slight markup, of course." Randy put his hand into his coat pocket, crinkled the bag loud enough for Kevin to hear it. "I need a hit, man, I can't wait to smoke this stuff."

"Let's at least wait 'till we get to my house," Kevin said.

"Don't be such a wuss, Kev," Randy said. "Nobody cares about a little bud. The stuff's legal now."

They had reached the alley behind Kevin's house on Grove Street. The alley was demarcated by a variety of fences that divided his neighbors' back yards. They walked past his next-door neighbor's yard, which had a simple four-foot chain-link fence. This stopped at his own back yard, which had a more solid wood slat fence. They stopped outside the back gate, where three garbage cans sat waiting for pickup. Kevin himself had recently placed two large concrete bricks next to the fence, making a convenient place to sit and hide away from the world inside his house. He'd scoped this spot out long ago. All the neighbors across the alley had wood fences, making it difficult for them to see his hiding place that easily.

"Screw you, man," Kevin said. "Let's roll a blunt, I need a hit, too."

He and Randy grabbed a seat on those bricks. Randy pulled out the baggie. "I left all my bongs at home; we'll have to settle for rolling our own." He pulled from another pocket a small packet of cigarillos in a bright red and yellow package. "I got these from a guy at school." Kevin watched as he expertly slit open one cigarillo with a pocketknife and slid a thumb through to dump the tobacco onto the ground. He pulled a bud from the baggie and began to crumble it into the now empty cigarillo paper. Randy had been smoking a little longer than his buddy, and when he licked the paper to seal it, he held up a tightly rolled blunt. He held it up with pride for Kevin to see. Kevin snatched it from his hand. He ran the blunt under his nose, making a show of smelling it. He didn't care how silly it might look. He just wanted to get loaded.

They lit up. Kevin went first, sucked in a lungful and held it, but couldn't help a cough after a few seconds. Randy took the blunt and leaned back against the fence. He drew a long drag, closed his eyes and blew a steady stream of smoke out. Kevin eyed him for a second, then the blunt, and emulated him, closing his eyes. He let his problems drain away, his less than perfect home life, issues at school, all of it. Even that pesky conscience.

* * *

The arrest did not take long. Steve and Suzy booked the robbery suspect into County Jail, at the top floor of the San Francisco Hall of Justice. The building used to be the headquarters of the San Francisco Police Department, but in 2015, SFPD had moved into a new building at Mission Rock, down near AT&T Park.

They finished booking their robbery suspect. When they emerged together, it was after ten a.m. They returned to Steve's vehicle, a black SUV, parked in a fenced lot behind the building along Bryant Street. He drove out and down the street and made the turn onto 4th Street toward AT&T Park. Mission Rock was just moments away from the Hall of Justice. He pulled into the giant parking lot that stretched between McCovey Cove and the police headquarters building. He parked near Suzy's pickup truck.

"That was fun," Suzy said. "It's always good to fight crime on my day off."

"Would a sincere 'thank you' lighten your mood?" Steve asked with a smile.

"Breakfast would lighten it more."

"Rain check, please, and I'll pencil you in with permanent ink. This whole thing has got my brain going and I want to get to work."

He suddenly became aware of the look in her eye, one of mild regret, and he quickly shared that regret. "See you tonight?"

She stopped short of giving her boyfriend a good-bye kiss in front of the station. "Good luck," she said with an anticipatory smile and slipped away.

Steve entered the building through a back door. He rode the elevator up to the Homicide section. There, he sought out the office of Captain John Stanson. Stanson was Captain of Inspectors, but rather than have an office amongst other brass, he made his home in the heart of the plainclothes force, where he actually was a part of the effort to fight crime. He oversaw numerous plainclothes units, including the Homicide Division. He was also the brainchild behind the reactivation of Steve's unit, simply called "Special Forces."

Stanson had been Steve's mentor as he came up through the ranks and distinguished himself. Few people on the force knew that their relationship actually went back more years than Steve had been a cop.

Steve made his way through the Homicide section, nodding to several Inspectors that he knew and worked with. He locked eyes with Stanson through his office window as he crossed the room. Steve slipped quietly into the office and closed the door. He was one of few people who had permission to impose on the Captain like this.

"What did you think of my arrest this morning?" Steve asked.

"I read the report narrative you sent from your phone. It took me a minute to stop laughing." Even now, Stanson let a grin crease a face that was starting to show its age. Stanson was not quite six feet tall, in his mid-fifties, and his hairline had receded.

"I want to tackle the marijuana problem in this city," Steve said.

Stanson fell silent, leaning back in his chair as he digested this. "That's a big bite, son. The legalization marijuana is a loaded issue right now."

"It's getting to be a bigger problem than anyone wants to acknowledge."

"I know. But as much as you hate it, there are politics to consider. Federal law still prohibits it, but medicinal marijuana has been legalized here in

California."

Steve smirked at this. "You know as well as I do that most of the marijuana out there is not being used as 'medicinal.' That's what I want to go after." He huffed. "Look, I get it; it's about to be legal. But there are still rules and those that partake need to be reminded of that. Plus, they've been lulled into a false sense of security because the department quit enforcing pot laws. That's to our detriment and I want to change that, at least for a while."

"California voters elected to legalize for recreational use, and that takes effect next week, January 1st. What can you do between now and then?"

"I've got some ideas."

Stanson went silent again for a moment to consider what Blazer said. "Son, I respect the hell out of the fact that you are such an anti-drug crusader. Does this have anything to do with your South American rotation during your Green Beret days?"

"Only in the sense that that period of my life helped cement my anti-drug belief. I was a pit bull when I went after the cartels in Colombia. And yeah, that little war carried over into Miami when I left the service. Some cartel wet workers found me and tried to take me out, so I took the war to them."

"You were lucky you had a good working relationship with the local DEA and that they bailed you out. Just keep in mind, you play by a different set of rules here. You're talking specifically about marijuana. The politics I was referring to is the fact that too much of the public is willing to excuse it."

"I'm hoping to shine a light on the parts that the public doesn't see. Maybe I can change a little public opinion. In the meantime, I'm itching to get some dope off the street."

"You got a plan?"

Movement outside the window caught the attention of both, a plainclothes cop approaching the office. Steve nodded toward him. "I asked Lieutenant Cameron to join us, I may be asking his assistance with some of this."

Steve held the door open for Lieutenant George Cameron. "Thanks for coming, LT," he said.

"Captain," Cameron nodded to Stanson. Cameron was about Stanson's height, with a slightly scruffy appearance and short graying hair. "What's going on, Blazer?"

"For starters," Steve said, "Tell me what you think about Prop 64."

"Legalizing the mari-ju-wanna?" He caught Steve's quizzical look. "That's what we call it, the running joke in my squad. For starters, legalizing is a bad idea. Too many people are down and out as it is, and if we legalize it, we'll see a whole lot more than that. I know the former Governor downgraded the penalties for possession. An ounce no longer buys you a court case, just a simple fine. That may generate some quick cash here and there. Trouble is, it doesn't get someone any more consequences. Cases about just marijuana are not as prevalent as people think."

"That is one of the talking points that pro-pot people use," Steve said. "Supposedly, there's a huge population in jails and prisons of people who just had some pot. The reality is, for years, DAs have prosecuted marijuana cases less and less, so cops push those cases less and less. The number of cases in the system for simple possession is not what the activists think it is. Possession for sale is a different story."

"What do you got going on, Blazer?" Cameron asked.

"I'm looking to take some dope off the street," Steve said. "I want to tackle the problem of illegal marijuana. Someone's got to take on the political crap surrounding it. I really think I can save some lives if I do this."

"Save some lives? That's a tall order. I have a hunch that the powers that be won't like it. I'll back you, though. A couple guys on my squad have bought into the hype about taxing it, but they'll back me if it comes down to it."

To Stanson, Steve said, "I'd like to assemble my guys from Special Forces for this, unofficially if necessary."

"No, I'll sign off on it. How are you going to do this?" Stanson asked.

"I'm still working on that. For starters, I can have a couple of my guys start checking with some precincts about tips on houses with suspicious activity. They can look for anything that could add up to a marijuana grow."

"Sarge, if that's what you want, I got plenty of those," Cameron brought up. "We compile those reports for future use. I've got a list of possible grow houses I've been sitting on for a while."

Steve stood up. "Give the list to me."

CHAPTER 3

Two vehicles rolled into the Richmond District that afternoon. At one p.m., traffic on 22nd Street was minimal. This was a residential neighborhood and most residences were quiet. Kids were off attending classes at several nearby schools and parents were in the city at their jobs. There were a few older residents out tending to their yards or walking their dogs. He saw a handful of pedestrians on sidewalks. Steve took all this in as he drove through, examining the neighborhood.

Seated in the passenger seat of Steve's SUV was the unofficial second in command of the Special Forces unit, Inspector Scot Black. Like each member of the team, Black had his own area of expertise. Black had been recruited from the Asian Crimes Task Force. As a child, he'd traveled throughout the Orient, a Caucasian immersed in Asian cultures. He spoke several of the languages. Along with his knowledge of the cultures, he'd trained in several of the martial arts. He didn't claim to be a Buddhist, but he believed in several of the traditions. Scot tried to remain a man of peace, even as the world around him became increasingly less peaceful. This was a trait that Steve sought out when he recruited Black. Too many people thought Steve was a cop who operated outside the law and the history of the Special Forces unit was surrounded by a reputation of lawlessness. Steve had every intention of keeping the unit legit, and he purposefully brought Scot in as his own personal watch dog. Scot did not relish the idea at first, but he had settled into the unit and found real purpose in what they did.

Steve drove through the block checking address-es until he found the right one. Once he found it, he examined the house as he drove by. At several other houses on this block, he found people outside, working in their yard, watering lawns, walking dogs, working on cars in the driveway—here there was no activity. He saw that every window had not only a closed set of blinds, but no gaps around those blinds, as if they were sealed off. The yard was slightly brown, as if it had not been cared for in a while. There was no vehicle in the driveway. The house was quiet and unassuming.

At the end of the block, Steve pulled a U-turn and stopped at the curb. He grabbed the small push-to-talk radio phone—along with a police scanner, on which the volume was turned down, Blazer had set up a private frequency for the push-to-talk radios between himself and his team. He keyed the button on the side, which connected him to the second vehicle used by his team. He could see that vehicle at the end of the block he'd just come from. "There should be an alley behind this block. You guys check the back and see if there is any activity."

* * *

In the other vehicle, a dark blue unmarked Ford Crown Victoria sedan, Dave Castillo picked up the radio as A.J. Miano got the car underway. "Wild Boy Four, copy."

A.J. drove them slowly up the next block of 22nd Street. As he pulled past a neighbor's house with a tall wooden fence and into the alley, he gave his partner a cryptic glance. Miano was a third generation Italian American. He'd served in the military and then joined the police department. A.J. had demolitions training in the Army, which led to a tour with the SFPD Bomb Squad. Steve recruited him into the new Special Forces during a fateful drug case, and he saw that Blazer was on a crusade against crime. For this, he had Miano's respect.

A.J. stopped the car and let his partner out. Dave jumped from the car and padded up the alley, along the fences that bordered backyards. Most of the fences were only five to six feet tall, and he was able to glance over, checking yards until he reached the address the team was interested in. A.J. followed along in their vehicle just a few feet behind him.

Dave Castillo was another cop with a particular skill and mindset born of his upbringing. Dave had grown up in tough ethnic neighborhoods in East Bay. He was a child of divorce, which opened the door to acting out, which led to exposure to a local Latino gang. He flirted with the gang lifestyle, but decided as a teenager that he didn't really fit in. While the older kids were out slinging dope and committing petty crimes, Dave figured out he was too shy to be so assertive. He distanced himself from the gangs, though he still remained friends with some of them, at least the ones who survived and did not end up in prison. He joined the Army right out of high school, and despite being a quiet guy, ended up in the Rangers. He then joined the Military Police for a short time before transferring to the Reserves. He found something of a purpose in a life of adventure and service, so he began taking criminal justice classes, and found his way into the SFPD Police Academy. While the first half of his twenties was spent in the Army, the second half was spent on the police force. After a year in patrol, he joined the SWAT team, and because of his past, worked with a gang suppression unit. He was also a veteran of George Cameron's Vice Squad, which was where Blazer had recruited him. He'd gone back to Vice following their previous case until Blazer and Special Forces called him away again today.

Dave reached the corner of fence that surrounded the yard of their target house. He paused there, scoping out the yard. He saw no movement, no one outside, heard no noise from the house. He backed away for a moment and reached into the car for a pair of binoculars. He returned to the fence and lensed the façade, checking windows.

A.J. killed the engine and crept up next to him. Without taking his binos off the house, Dave held out his hand, saying simply, "Radio." Miano handed over the push-to-talk. Dave keyed the transmit button. "Wild Boy One, Four."

"One, go," was Blazer's quick response.

"Scoping the back, I see no movement. I'm looking at the windows, I can see what looks like foil on the inside, or maybe paint."

"Stand by and keep over-watch," Steve replied.

* * *

Blazer had driven back into the street and back past the target house, and they once again examined the grounds to check for any signs of occupancy. Steve pulled another U-turn at the end of the block. He decided it provided a better vantage point.

He soon saw another potential problem. With

some of the neighbors were out, a few had noticed the SUV driving from one end of the block more than once and were now giving the vehicle a curious and concerned look. For the moment, Steve debated internally what he should do about this, but he supposed it was time to do some investigating.

"We've pretty much figured that no one is home," he said to Scot. "If there's a grow inside, it could be that our green-thumbers think they can leave it unattended. So, if they're not home, we don't need to worry about being too secret. Why don't you go talk to the neighbors and see if they know who they're living next to?"

When Scot stepped out, Steve fished out his cell phone. He quickly looked up on the internet a customer service number for a San Francisco based power company. He called them and surfed through their automated menu until he found a prompt that let him speak with an actual live person. "Yes, my name is Sergeant Steve Blazer, I'm with the San Francisco Police Department." He gave his badge number. "I'm looking for the power records for a residence in the Richmond District."

The rep was polite, but less than cooperative. "I'm sorry, Sergeant, I would need a court order to release that information. We consider our clients' confidentiality very important."

"Ma'am, I have reason to believe that this residence is the center of a major drug operation, and I'm a little pressed for time. Ironically, the power information could turn out to be crucial in getting a search warrant for the property."

"I'm very sorry, Sergeant, I cannot give out that information, but I would be happy to if you'll present my supervisor with a court order."

Steve pretended to relent. "OK, I'll work on getting that order. I'll get back to you." He hung up and went to work thinking up a new tactic.

* * *

Meanwhile, Scot Black approached a house two doors down from the target house. Like Blazer, he had also seen the eyes of the neighborhood watching them suspiciously. This first house had an older man, white haired and in his sixties, pruning branches from a small apple tree out front. As he approached, the man stopped what he was doing to size up the stranger.

"Afternoon, sir, I'm Inspector Black with the San Francisco Police." He presented his badge.

The old-timer calmed down visibly. "What can I do for you, Inspector?"

"Do you know who lives in the house just down the street?"

"You must be asking about the one two doors down." Scot nodded. "You know, I can't say I really know. That house has been vacant for a while, but I have seen some activity there the last few weeks. I think it might be rented out."

"Do you know the owners, or the people who rented it?"

"I met the owner a few times, long ago. Seemed nice enough."

"You said you'd seen some activity there recently?"

"It hasn't been a hustle and bustle, mind you. But in the last few weeks, I've seen some people in and out. Not much, but maybe once a week, I'll see a white van park there, and one or two young men go inside. Sometimes I'll see them smoking outside. They're never there very long."

"Could you describe them?"

The man waved this off. "I never got a very good look. They might have been Asian, might have been Hispanic."

"How about the car?" Scot persisted.

"I never really took much interest in that either, just that it was a white van."

* * *

Back in his truck, Steve dialed the power company again, and he hoped he would not recognize the voice as the same CSR he'd just spoken to. This time he reached a male rep. He avoided giving his name at the beginning. "Yes, hi, I have a rental property out in the Richmond District. I got some tenants in there now that I think are shady, and I'd like to check their power usage."

"What's the name on the account, sir?"

"That's the thing, sir, I think the name they gave me was fake. I think they may be running a drug ring there. I'd like to see if they're using an excessive amount of power for that. I want to get all my ducks in a row before I bring the law into it."

"I understand, sir." If nothing else, these CSRs were incredibly polite, Steve noticed. "Do you have the account number?"

Steve flinched loud enough for the man to hear him over the phone, trying to convey frustration. "No, as I said, all I have is the address."

"I can get the information from that."

Steve gave him the address, hoping he'd found his way around their system.

There was a long tense pause. "Hmm," the man finally said, "there does seem to be a lot of power going to this house. Wait a minute." Steve could hear the man tapping his keyboard. "I found a flag on this file. We have Smart meters set up in that area, and it looks like the meter detected an anomaly. It sent an automatic request to be serviced by a technician. That technician was there just a week ago, and he made some observations about the meter. It looked like it had been tampered with, but he couldn't tell how. He made a notation to have it investigated. We have a backlog of service requests, so it has not been investigated yet."

Steve raised his eyebrows at this. Still playing the part of the in-the-dark landlord, he said, "That does it, I'll have to get my lawyer involved with these guys. Thank you for your help."

Steve hung up and thought for a moment. He grabbed the radio and keyed it. "One to Four, any movement?"

Dave answered, "Negative."

Moments later, Scot returned to the SUV. "I get the same story from every neighbor. They all seem to think the house has been rented, and they see traffic there maybe once a week, but they've never met the neighbors. Can't identify ethnicity. They do say they've seen the same white van."

"I managed to get some info from the power company," Steve said. "A Smart meter technician reported possible tampering a week ago, but it hasn't been checked yet."

"So, what now?"

"Now, we call a Judge." Steve palmed his phone and punched in a number. When an operator answered, identifying the number as the courthouse, Steve gave his name, rank and badge number and said, "I need to speak with the on-duty judge."

Moments later, he was speaking with that Judge's clerk, who put him through to, "Judge Wahl."

"Your Honor, this is Sergeant Steve Blazer, SFPD. I'm requesting a Search Warrant for a house in the Richmond District. We're looking for a major marijuana grow."

"Probable cause?" Steve could already hear skepticism in the Judge's voice.

"Our department got an anonymous tip several days ago. Neighbors have seen suspicious traffic at the house, and the power meter has been reported as tampered with."

"That's a little flimsy."

"I realize that, sir, but we need to act on this quick—"

"Sergeant, I can't authorize a warrant for the possibility of a couple of lousy plants based on hearsay about traffic that a reasonable person may or may not find suspicious. We're in the wrong political climate to go after a few marijuana plants. I'm sorry, I will not authorize a search warrant." The judge hung up.

Scot's eyes were on him. Dave and A.J. waited at the back of the house.

For a moment, Steve reflected on the reason he had brought Scot onto his team. Right now, Blazer wanted very badly to kick down the door to this house and verify what he felt more and more strongly, that marijuana plants were growing inside. But without the law behind him, he would become what the rest of the department already assumed about him, and what he himself did not want—that he was a cop with over the top methods of getting the job done, methods that jeopardized his cases and tarnished the shield. Scot was brought onto the team to keep him in check, but also to remind himself and others that he was not out to stop the bad guys no matter the cost, but to uphold the law.

"What do you think?" he asked. "Do you suspect that there's weed in that house?"

"I think it's there," Scot said. "But the question before the court is, do we have enough to lawfully enter and see?"

"We don't have enough for an exigent circumstances entry," Steve said. "And short of the place suddenly spewing smoke..." He let that thought trail off.

Steve shook his head. "Let me try one more judge. Judge Allen helped us with the Orozco drug case last time. I got the sense that he's almost as much a crusader as I am." He was dialing as he spoke, and his call was answered. "Judge Allen, please. This is Sergeant Steve Blazer, SFPD."

The judge was on the phone in moments. "Your honor? Sergeant Steve Blazer, I hope you remember me."

"Yes, I do, Sergeant, how's the department treating you?"

"Busy as ever, and in fact that's why I'm calling. I'm requesting a search warrant for a house that we suspect has a large drug operation." He was careful to not yet specify the kind of drugs suspected to be present. He knew he would have to—warrants had to be specific in what the police were there to search for.

"Tell me what you're looking for," the Judge said.

Steve took a breath. "We're investigating tips regarding a large illegal marijuana grow." He described their probable cause, as he had for Judge Wahl. "What I'm expecting, your honor, is to walk into this house and find wall to wall plants. Based on their power consumption and the meter being tampered with, I believe we'll find just that."

Scot listened with bated breath, but Steve's end of the conversation was limited to simple 'yes' answers for a moment. Steve finally said, "Yes, sir, thank you." He tapped his phone and said, "We got it. He's emailing me the affidavit for my electronic signature."

Steve grabbed the radio. "Get ready and stand by, we're going in."

"Ten-four," Dave responded.

They left the SUV and went to the back. Steve opened his back hatch and pulled out a pile of tactical vests. They were Kevlar vests with black covers, with the word "Police" emblazoned on the back, as well as patches in the shape of the SFPD star attached to the front. The vests had pouches for things like grenades, in whatever model needed for the job, but those pouches would remain empty. Both Steve and Scot pulled their department issue SIG Sauer P229s to check their load.

As soon as he'd holstered, Steve's phone vibrated—the warrant had been emailed. He checked it over, clicked a signature to it and pocketed his phone.

Steve opened a small weapons locker he kept under the floorboard of the back area. Scot saw this and couldn't resist a joke. "Most people keep a spare tire there."

Instead, Steve pulled out a twelve-gauge riot shotgun. He checked the safety and thumbed in several shells. "No one is home, but we go in hard anyway. Ready?"

He received a nod. Steve went quickly to his front seat and grabbed the radio once again. Glancing at his watch, he radioed, "Moving in. Entry in one minute."

* * *

At the back fence, the wait had seemed endless for Dave and A.J. For a while they felt like they'd been forgotten. Maintaining their surveillance, they were not privy to what was going on up front, interviewing neighbors and seeking the warrant. With the endless waiting, the call to action was sudden and sent nerves jumping.

"Ten-four," Dave acknowledged Steve's last order. He and A.J. had also retrieved their tactical vests, doing it one at a time to maintain the surveillance.

A.J. now poised at the fence with his partner.

"It won't take us long to cross the yard. In thirty seconds, we hop the fence."

"You know it," Dave said.

* * *

Out front, the Special Forces cops bolted from behind the black SUV. They ran past three houses, past neighbors who gaped at the tactical vests and the openly carried weapons. Scot took a moment to motion frantically to anyone along their route to go inside.

Steve reached the porch, and only now took into account the structure of the front door. There was no screen, and the door looked solid but penetrable. It appeared standard enough that it would yield to a swift kick. If need be, he could blast the lock or even the hinges with his shotgun.

They positioned themselves on either side of the door. When Steve saw that Scot was in position, he reached over and pounded on the door. "Police! Search warrant!" He waited, counting in his head.

They received no answer from inside. He stepped back and kicked hard at the door. His foot landed next to the knob, and it smashed inward. Steve lunged in after it, his shotgun leading the way. "Police!" he shouted.

They walked into a jungle. Immediately in the room, they found no furniture, just wall to wall plants. Steve stopped just inside the doorway to look at what he had found. Another crash and a shout at the back door—Dave and A.J. entering. The team filtered into the rest of the house to check for any human occupants. In one minute, they gathered once again in the front room.

"House is empty," Scot reported.

"And there's plants everywhere," Dave added.

Steve was shaking his head as he looked over the front room. "Let's take a look."

The house was a two bedroom, but was obviously not lived in. They found rows of marijuana stalks, most around five feet tall. The ones in the front room were taller, indicating they would be harvested next. Rows of plants in one of the bedrooms were still only a couple feet tall. In every room, each plant was in its own pot, really a plastic bucket filled with soil. Each room had a row of heating lights hanging precariously from the ceiling at about eye level. Bundles of extension cord from these lights extended back to plug strips, which they found plugged into every outlet in the house. They also found black tubes stretched across each row of plants in every room. These they found attached to faucets in the kitchen and bathrooms, a watering system. They found an electronic timer system attached to it; the kind people use on their yard sprinklers. In checking out the network of hoses, they found that some of the extension cords ran down the hallways, and were bundled together with the water tubes, creating an electrical hazard. Dave took it upon himself to count the plants and came up with a count of two hundred fifty.

With a great feeling of satisfaction, Steve went to the front door to make two phone calls, one to George Cameron, and the second to Captain Stanson.

* * *

In ten minutes, the area was swarming with cops and the investigation stretched for hours. Police vehicles, marked and unmarked, lined the streets. Neighbors from the entire block had come to view the commotion and the yard had been taped off. Inspectors from Special Forces and Vice had done a careful job of examining and photographing everything in the house, including the power meter tampering on the outside. Each plant was numbered and photographed. Steve in particular searched the house for any kind of paperwork related to the owner. He did find a plastic sheaf full of papers in a plant-filled garage, some kind of rental agreement. He found a phone number on the top of the first page, that of a property management company. He jumped on the phone while officers carried plants outside. The stalks were uprooted from their plastic bucket-planters and loaded into a pickup truck driven by one of Cameron's men. Steve planned to personally verify their destruction. For a moment, he looked around at some of the neighbors, seeing a marijuana grow disassembled from a house on their block. He wondered what each person's reaction was. Shock at seeing such crime and stupidity in their neighborhood? Sadness that good and "harmless" weed was going to waste? Considering the prevalent softening of attitudes, he figured it was probably a mixture of both.

Steve finally hung up his phone. Cameron and Stanson were talking nearby, and Steve approached. The Captain looked at him expectantly. "I managed to track down the owner of the home, a property management company. I worked my way up the chain of command and got handed to some executive vice president. He was actually surprised that the house was being used this way, and he swears up and down that the management company had no idea. He wants to fully cooperate, so he will come in for an interview, I imagine with lawyers in tow."

"You think he's being truthful about not knowing?" Stanson asked.

Steve put his sarcasm and cynicism aside. "Yeah, I do. He says he's going to dig up some names for who rented the house. It would not surprise me if the names were fake, or even stolen identities. I guess the courts will decide if they need to seize the house in conjunction with the felony." Steve sighed as he stared off to the west. Clouds were gathering, and a storm was coming in. "I tried to gauge his attitude, but I could have guessed wrong."

"Is that going to make a difference?" Cameron asked.

"I think so. It will be a measure of how cooperative the guy is going to be. If he supports legalization, if he sees a few plants as no big deal, he'll hide behind his lawyers and give us nothing. On the other hand, he'll be more forthcoming if—"

"If he agrees with you," Cameron grinned.

Steve returned the grin part way. "Can it, LT, I've heard all the jokes about me being a control freak."

Stanson nodded toward the street. "The media is here."

Steve looked at the news van stopping up the block, just outside the line of police vehicles. The van bore the logo of a local TV station and had the erectable antenna mounted on top. A camera man stepped out and scoped the scene as he started to set up a shoulder mounted camera.

Steve's face darkened. "I'm not talking to them," he announced. "I think I should stay low-key for a while."

"I'll take care of it," Stanson said.

"Besides," Steve nodded to Cameron, "I want to check out a few more locations on your list." He left to gather his team.

* * *

Kevin entered the alley behind his house. His walk from school was just a few blocks, no big deal. But now that he was in the alley, away from most prying eyes on the street, he fished the pack of cigarettes from his backpack. As he lit one up, he suddenly realized how cold it was and pulled his sweatshirt a little tighter. He took a deep drag on the cigarette and blew out a cloud. He stopped next to the back-yard gate in his hiding place to finish his cigarette. He used to worry that his parents would smell the smoke on him. But, he realized, both his parents smoked—

Their voices reached him from the house. They were fighting again. He took another drag on the cigarette, not eager to walk into the house.

The shouting in the house eased for a moment. He flicked his butt carelessly across the alley without bothering to stub it out. He wrenched open the gate and headed for the house.

"I'm tired of eating nothing but sandwiches," his mom was complaining.

"Maybe if you put your mind to it and put the bottle aside for five minutes," his Dad returned, "this whole family could have a decent meal. Come on, Nora."

"I get up at five o'clock every morning to go sling hash at that diner. The last thing I want to do when I get home is cook for you."

It was the usual shit. Kevin walked in the back door and headed straight for the hall leading to his room.

"Kevin, we need to talk to you, son," his dad called out.

Kevin considered just going on to his room and slamming the door. Instead, he sighed and went to the living room.

The living room was choked with cigarette smoke. Mom's cigarette sat burning away in an ash-tray on the end table next to her easy chair. His dad stood near the front door, his cigarette dangling from his mouth. He was on permanent disability after a work accident several years ago. He was shabbily dressed, jeans and a stained wife-beater and his hair was scraggly brown. His mom lounged in her tattered green easy chair. A bottle of Jack Daniels sat next to her ash tray. She had been pretty years ago, but decades of abuse to herself, drinking and smoking, had ravaged her looks. All of it made for an unhappy home.

"Your school called today, son," his Dad said. "They say you ditched your first three classes. Your principal says your history teacher is concerned that you're failing his class."

Kevin let his face take on a blank look. The fight he had heard appeared to have calmed, but the tension was still very apparent.

"Oh, leave the boy alone, Ted," his Mom said. "Who gives a damn about history anyway?"

"Nora, I want the boy to do better in school, and I think you do, too."

"Look, it's not my fault," Kevin burst out. "The teacher hates me; he's always riding my ass about stuff."

"If he hates you so much, why is he concerned enough to tell us about it?"

"Maybe if you didn't cut school so damn much," his mother muttered. She dragged on her cigarette.

"Why are you cutting school, son?" Ted asked, much calmer than Nora was.

"I ditched, like, one time," Kevin insisted. "It's no big deal."

"It is a big deal, Kevin. You're at a point in life where decisions can be critical. Everything you do has consequences, even if you don't see them."

"Whatever." Kevin dismissed him and turned to leave.

"This is not a whatever situation, Kevin. You're grounded for a week."

"Why?" Kevin demanded.

His dad's voice was getting angry again. "For ditching school. It was more than one time. I think you can use this week to work on some of your schoolwork and bring those grades back up."

"Whatever." Kevin gave up talking to them. He turned to leave the room.

"You're too hard on the boy, Ted," he heard his mother say. He stopped in the hallway, out of sight, to listen for a moment.

"Nora, I don't want him ending up like I did."

"Shit, you and I used to ditch school all the time."

"And look where it got us."

"Screw you, you son of a bitch!" Kevin heard a small crash. That would be his Mom throwing the ash tray at his Dad.

Kevin left and went to his room. He flopped onto his bed, and just lay there, trying to drown out the shouting voices outside. He slipped in a pair of earbuds, which were plugged into his cell phone. He surfed his music selection there and picked a rap song.

His dad was a total hypocrite. He wanted to lecture his son on life when his life was shit, by his own admission. He never really gave much thought to what his life could possibly hold for him. He didn't feel like starting to think about it now.

Kevin got up and waded through the mess of clothes and discarded electrical cords and forgotten sports equipment toward his window. Behind a dresser next to the window, there was a small hole in the wall—it had been there for years, the house was falling apart around the family. It had become a convenient place to hide his stash. He pulled out his baggie and quickly rolled a blunt. His face twisted at the fact that he still couldn't roll one as tight as Randy. He grabbed a lighter off the top of his dresser—his parents didn't come into his domain very often and had never questioned why he needed a lighter. He slid the window aside and sat perched on the sill. He lit the blunt and dragged deep, holding the smoke in his lungs to let the THC take effect. He let his left hand holding the blunt dangle out the window out of sight from the doorway. When he finally exhaled, he blew smoke out into the back yard.

His parents yelling had subsided but then started up again. He sighed and took another drag, feeling his brain drain. This was what his life had sunk to.

* * *

Steve yawned as he stepped off the elevator and headed toward Captain Stanson's office. His mentor was just hanging up the phone. Steve walked in and flopped onto a couch to one side. Despite his exhaustion, he let a satisfied smile draw at his face, and he made no effort to hide it. "We found a second grow house not six blocks from the first one. Same situation, rented house, but no apparent occupants. Three hundred plants. I just escorted the plants down to the evidence warehouse."

Stanson leaned back in his chair. "Years ago, I would have thought this was a part of a sophisticated drug network."

"That's the thing, Cap, it's the exact opposite. It's the average joe, your freaking neighbor. Everyone thinks this shit is so harmless, that it should be legalized and normalized. Information is out there on the net, how to grow it, ways to navigate the legal system. I won't just sit by and let that go unanswered."

"I'll tell you, son, not everyone in this town is a dope fiend," Stanson said. "The first bust made the five o'clock news. I just got word, call center supervisor reports that we've had dozens of new tips of possible grows all over this city, and even a couple in the East Bay."

"If I can get a list of addresses," Steve said, "I can compare it to Cameron's intel." Steve's phone rang and he pulled it out of a coat pocket. "Blazer. What's up, LT?" He glanced at Stanson as he listened. "I'll be right there." He ended the call. To Stanson, he said, "Cameron just got a call from the Fire Department. They're at a structure fire in North Potrero. They found another grow house."

* * *

Steve elected to let his team take the rest of the night off. He drove to Potrero Hill to meet up with Lieutenant Cameron and the fire department. He hadn't yet decided if he would push to take over the investigation, or maybe let Cameron handle it, or even the fire department's arson investigation team. He had to see what they were dealing with first. But the bottom line was, even if the plants were destroyed by the fire, he was content that more drugs were off the street.

The rain had started in earnest when he turned onto Southern Heights Avenue. Police patrol vehicles had blocked off the street, and he parked at the curb nearby. He carried his badge on a small chain around his neck, tucked into his shirt. He pulled it out and made sure it dangled in a visible spot, but then pulled his coat closed against the rain. The officer manning this barricade from his vehicle knew him, nodded and waved him through. Steve walked up the block, surveying what he saw.

Two fire engines were parked in front of a mid-size bungalow. Red and white lights lit the night, resulting in a surreal strobe against the backdrop of the rain. It had the weird effect of casting a spotlight on each character moving through the scene, as if everyone moved alone. The water on the ground was a mixture of rain and hose spray. Fire hoses stretched everywhere leading from the trucks up to the house, as well as one massive tube connecting a truck to a nearby hydrant. As he got closer, the smell hit him, the pungent odor of charred wood and smoke. He thought for a moment he smelled the odor of marijuana smoke, but that might just have been his imagination anticipating.

He stopped at the sidewalk in front of the house to survey the damage. The façade was blackened and torn up. He could see through gaps in the wall where sheetrock had been burned away or ripped into by fireman's tools. Inside the house, he saw the frenetic movement of flashlight beams, adding to the psychedelic atmosphere. He also spotted two firemen on the roof, their ladder nearby, chopping holes to vent smoke and check for embers. Overall, the fire appeared to be out, the scene safe. Some members of the crew were rolling hoses and packing to leave.

Steve happened to glance back and found George Cameron approaching. "Where's the rest of Special Forces?" Cameron asked.

"I gave them the night off. I'd like to see what we have here before I plunge everyone into another case."

"My guys too. I guess we're the schmucks with no life that can't let the job go."

Steve flagged down a passing firefighter. "SFPD. Where's the incident commander?"

The fire fighter pointed to a cluster of men standing next to a nearby engine. One held a radio as he spoke with the other two. A second man wore plain clothes, jeans and a fire department polo shirt. He was gesturing toward the house as the cops approached.

"Sergeant Blazer, Lieutenant Cameron, SFPD,"

Steve introduced them. "One of you called the department about this incident?"

"I did," the man with the radio said. His hair was white, including a droopy mustache. He was much shorter than Blazer but had a solid stocky build. "I'm Battalion Chief Riggins. This here is Sergeant Greendahl, the arson investigator." Greendahl simply waved to the cops, and Riggins went on. "Let me show you what we found."

He led the way up to the house. Blazer and Cameron maneuvered carefully around the hoses. Riggins stepped through the charred doorway with the mindset that a little soot and water would not kill anyone. Cameron was more careful to avoid getting ash on his clothes, but Blazer didn't care. He was already examining the scene, searching out what he knew he would find.

"Our guys made entry with hoses wide open," Riggins said loudly enough to be heard over equipment being used to check for hot spots. "Barely in the door, and they all tripped over this." He pointed at a row of plastic buckets. The plants in the buckets were scorched or wilted, but they recognized marijuana stalks. Steve saw the partially melted remnants of rubber tubing draped over many of the buckets. He figured it to be a watering system like the ones he'd seen in the other grow houses. The smell of burning bud was more prevalent here, and Blazer pulled a handkerchief from his pocket to hold over his mouth. "I really hate that smell," he muttered.

He looked at Cameron. "Just like the other two." To Riggins, he said, "We busted two of these grow houses today, and I suspect we'll find them all over town."

"You'll like this," Greendahl spoke for the first time. He motioned them to follow him back outside. Greendahl was tall and thin, in his forties, with an almost gaunt, angular face. He led the group to the side of the house. There, he pulled out a bright LED flashlight and fired it up. The bright beam lit the wall and froze on an electrical meter. Steve immediately saw that the glass cover was gone.

"They tampered with it and rigged it to take on all the electrical for the lights inside. But someone did a piss poor job. Once the rain started falling, it shorted out and fried everything."

"My heart bleeds for their loss," Steve muttered.

He pulled Cameron aside. "LT, this can only help our investigation. Working off your list, we can check these locations for any tampering of the electrical."

"We'll need warrants for each location," Cameron said.

"Leave that to me. I found an in with my first bust this morning. But I know we can't oversell this. We get the warrant, but we tell the judge, if there's no power issues, we walk away and don't make entry. Nobody's rights are violated. But with the warrant, any tampering we find validates the warrant, and we can make entry and act on what we find."

Cameron was smiling. "Then let's regroup tomorrow and do this."

CHAPTER 4

On his way to work the next morning, Steve received a call from Stanson. He'd intended to immediately deliver the paper affidavits that Judge Allen had requested for their telephone warrant yesterday. Instead, Stanson diverted him to an address in the Mission District for what the Captain told him was a "459 right up your alley." Why was Stanson being so mysterious about a 459, a simple burglary? Steve quickly sent a mass text to his team, giving them the address. He steered his SUV from north to east and headed across town.

He reached Sixteenth Street and found his crime scene. Two SFPD black and whites were parked outside, no lights on. Typically, a "cold" burglary was not an urgent crime. Though burglary was a felony, when the crime was long over, it could usually be delegated to a Community Services Officer, not a sworn cop, to take a simple report. This one was apparently serious enough to warrant a uniformed responder, as well as being referred to the Investigations Bureau, and now Special Forces. He was the first of his team to arrive, so he parked behind one patrol unit and surveyed the scene. A stretch of sidewalk had been taped off, and the usual gawkers stood outside the boundaries. He spotted a uniform, an officer he did not know, outside a non-descript door, speaking with an overweight security guard seated on a stool. He showed the officer his badge. "Sergeant Blazer, Special Forces. Looks like I caught this case. Can you run it for me?"

"Sure. Medical cannabis dispensary, they got burglarized sometime after two a.m."

Hearing this explained why Stanson had been so mysterious. Steve glanced over at the gawkers and wondered how many were customers of the shop. Then he wondered how many of their illnesses were legitimate.

"Primary officer is inside talking to the owner. Looks like a simple smash and grab, they busted out the glass door here in front. Some glass cases inside were also broken and some samples taken. The guy had a whole other stash locked up inside that the thieves couldn't get to. CSI is on the way to dust for prints."

"Thanks." Steve clapped him on the shoulder and headed for the door.

The security guard stood and said, "Ordinarily, I would have to buzz everyone in. But the door was left open."

Despite the glass shattered and in a pile on the sidewalk, the door was propped open. Steve stepped carefully around the bulk of the glass and entered the shop. He found himself in a cramped lobby and noted a small window and intercom speaker on a wall. The small lobby had no decorations or signs, just plain white walls. He remembered when dispensaries first started popping up ten years ago. For security reasons, in a place like this, the "patient" would simply place an order from a menu or book, using the intercom, and it was filled by the staff,

given through a security window. With the preva-
lence of the drug and the indifference of the public,
those security measures had gone very lax. Shops
like this were now run like any other retail store.
But he had to wonder... Most of these places did
still have a security guard...almost like they were
acknowledging that this harmless drug still had a
stigma attached to it.

Steve stepped into the main shop.

The smell of marijuana inside the shop hit him
and instantly infuriated him. He steeled himself and
scoped the interior. Another uniform was interviewing a Hispanic man who appeared to be in his
forties but had a grizzled face that made him look
older. Before interjecting himself into the interview,
Steve examined the layout of the shop. The lighting
was dim, and the main floor was open. Two walls
were lined with shelves and hangers showing off
everything from bongs to rolling papers to lighters.
There was even a section displaying pro-marijuana
T-shirts and bumper stickers. Before he got more
angry at this place that glamorized that which he
blamed for the downfall of society, he turned away
from the merchandise. He checked the countertops,
which were also glass. Many were shattered, leaving
more shards of glass scattered on the floor and the
shelves inside. Steve checked these counters and
found an example of what must have been taken.
He saw a single booklet inside, the size of a photo
album. It was open, and he saw a page lined with
clear plastic pouches. In the pouches, he saw bundles
of marijuana bud. Looking at the counter, he saw
this was where they displayed their wares. This was
the only booklet left.

Steve finally approached the shop owner and
the uniform. "Sergeant Blazer," he said, and then
directed his inquiries to the shop owner. "What's

your name, sir?"

"Charlie Garcia, I run this establishment." Garcia stood about five foot six and had a growing paunch to go with his grizzled face and receding hair line.

"I know you've spoken to the officer, but can you run down again for me what happened?"

"I was at home asleep around two when the alarm company called me. They confirmed that none of my employees—I only have two—should be at the shop. I came down and found all the glass shattered."

"What was taken?" Steve asked.

"Everything from the counters. I don't grow here and I keep most of my supply locked in my vault back here." He pointed to a heavy metal door with a keypad next to the knob. "It looks like they tried to open the vault but couldn't." He shook his head. "I can't believe this is happening to me, in this city of all places."

"What do you expect when you have something all the stoners want?" Steve grumbled.

Garcia glared at him. "Look, Officer, I deal in medical cannabis only. I don't have stoner customers. That will remain so until California allows Prop 64 to take effect."

Steve drew himself to his full height. "Sir, right now, the law legalizing marijuana has not taken effect. People may use it for medical purposes, and stoners may use the medical excuse to get high—you know as well as I do that this is most of the business of shops like this. In other words, you have stoner customers. But no matter how much denial the nation is in about harmful this shit really is, Federal Law still says marijuana is a banned substance. However, because this is California and because this is San Francisco, my department policy says I cannot arrest you as a drug dealer for all the contraband you peddle. In the business you're in, how do you *not* expect to be a target of criminals?"

"People steal valuable electronics all the time," Garcia said, "Should we ban all that too?"

"Electronics are not mind-altering substances," Steve answered.

Garcia scoffed. "That's debatable." He took a breath. "Look, Officer, we can debate the pros and cons till we're blue in the face. I try to run a legit medical care business here. I make all my customers sign a form that explains that they are in violation of federal law and they use at their own risk. I can at least acknowledge the law. Can you at least accept that?"

Steve took a breath. He softened, sensing that the shop owner was legitimately offering an olive branch. "In the interest of justice, how about we continue the interview." He glanced up at the wall and pointed up at a pair of dark pods. They almost blended into the ceiling. "Can you tell me about your surveillance system?"

Garcia glanced up at his ceiling. "I have a digital system in the back, it stores images. Come on, I'll show you."

He beckoned Blazer behind the counter and led him through the entrance to a hallway. They passed the vault door, and Steve gave it a glance, confirming scratch marks around the door latch and electronic keypad.

Garcia led him into an office. The walls were plain white, but there were printed pieces of art scattered haphazardly on the walls, all representing the marijuana leaf. Steve seethed at the sight. He turned his attention to a metal stand in the corner, with a black electronic unit sitting on it. "Hold on," Garcia said. "I have to hook my lap top up to it to view. I forgot it in the lobby. I take it home with me at night." He ducked out into the hallway.

"Jeez," Steve muttered to himself, "you're so scatterbrained, how much do you smoke?" He'd been sizing Garcia up since he met the man. He smelled of marijuana smoke, but considering his business, that wasn't so surprising, and it could be from anywhere. But Steve also noted that his pupils had dilated. The guy was high right now.

He glanced around the office, looking not at the art and décor but the business-related items on the desk. Could he spot some clue as to where the guy got his stash? If he did, what would he do with that information? He observed a strange sight next to the office phone, an old-school rolodex. It was open to a card with scribbling on it. Written in scribble were the initials B.A.W.G., and an address and phone number. He memorized the address, then fished out his cell phone. Lieutenant Cameron had texted him the list of address of possible grow houses. He compared the address to the list, but it was not there. If he found a moment, he would try to check out that address.

Garcia returned with a small notebook computer and a dangling cord. He set it next to the digital surveillance device and plugged in the cord. In moments, he had opened the program and was searching last night's footage. Steve leaned over his shoulder to watch.

The images were in black and white. Garcia fast forwarded through the night's footage, starting from when he locked up around 8pm. Steve watched the screen intently. Just after 2am, activity suddenly burst from the screen, and Garcia rewound the footage to the beginning. The camera showed the glass of the front door shattering, the glass shards reflecting white on the screen. Steve watched two subjects duck in through the door cleared of most of its glass. One carried a metal bar of some kind. He was easily able to pry open the inner door from the lobby to the sales area. The two began smashing the glass cases, and fumbling inside the cases. Items pulled out were placed into a black gym bag. While one subject attacked a second display case, his partner hopped a small gate to the space behind the counter. A second window on the screen showed him entering the room with the vault to examine the door.

Steve watched the footage intently, searching for any clues as to who he was looking at. The subjects were both of stocky build. They were covered head to toe in black, wearing black jeans and black hoodies with no logos on them. Hoods were pulled tight over their heads, and they never turned their faces to the camera. They wore gloves, so fingerprints were unlikely. The second man used a crowbar to try and pry open the door to the vault. After approximately two minutes of working on that door, his partner called out to him, silent on the screen, and they fled back out the front door.

Steve glanced up as members of his team filed into the office. "Can you rewind it for us?" he asked of Garcia.

The shop owner moved his mouse and clicked over the appropriate button. Scot, Dave and A.J. gathered around him and they watched the video through again. Before the end, Steve had Garcia pause it, just as their suspects were heading for the door.

Steve looked at his men. "Observations?" His eyes burned into them one by one.

When he reached Black, Scot said, "You really want one of us to say it out loud?"

Steve shrugged. "Someone has to."

Scot huffed. "Based on their body shape, body movement...I'd say they were both black."

"Not just that," Dave said, "they move like a couple of thugs."

"I was thinking the same thing for the same reason," Steve said. "Unfortunately, we can see no description beyond that. Unmarked clothing, no exposed skin, no visible tattoos, nothing seen of their faces. All in all, not much to go on."

He stared at the screen a moment, scrutinizing the image of the second crook headed for the door. Something about the video bothered him, some clue that he had not seen nibbled at his mind. He couldn't identify what was trying to jump out. "Run it again," he requested.

Garcia hit the button. The burglary began again. Steve watched the thugs hitting the glass cases. This time, he tried to ignore the one jumping the swinging gate and watched his partner. The guy swung his crowbar over and over, smashing four cases in a row. And suddenly Steve saw what had been bothering him.

The thug smashed the last case...and tossed the crowbar aside.

Steve was deep in thought as the rest of the video played out. When the screen went blank, Steve stepped away from the video system and out into the hallway. Curious, the rest of the team filed out after him.

Steve went back out to the lobby and stopped for a second at the entrance to the hallway. He glanced up at the camera in the corner, which had captured the burglary. He looked to his right, scanning the floor. He found what he was looking for, sitting in shadows in a corner of the walkway.

He'd seen the thug toss the crowbar into a corner behind the counter.

He caught the eye of a Crime Scene Investigator nearby taking pictures of the broken glass and beckoned the young man over. He shined a small flashlight down into the corner. "Make sure this item is logged, photographed and collected. You might be able to get some prints off it."

His team had gathered behind the counter to view the discovery. Steve looked at Garcia. "Your burglars wore gloves, so finding prints is a long shot. But we'll see what happens."

He drew Scot aside. "I'm going to stick here and wrap this up and I'll hit up the crime lab down at Hunter's Point. You guys head back to Mission Rock and start checking some of the suspected grow house locations. I want to be kicking down doors by 1300 Hours."

Steve tried to ignore the look in his partner's eye, the look that seemed to say, uh-oh, he used military time, he must be serious.

* * *

San Francisco Police Department was in the process of building a state-of-the-art crime lab at a site on Evans Avenue, which was just blocks from the current crime lab at Hunter's Point. Steve took the crowbar to the Hunter's Point building and met with a fingerprint tech. He stood by while the crowbar was dusted for prints. The CSI tech used a colored powder so any prints would show up against the black steel of the crowbar. They got lucky, finding a partial print near one end of the bar. The print was quickly scanned into the computer, and the computer did a search of databases for a match. In less than an hour, he was leaving the crime lab, now en route to the Haight Ashbury District. He had a suspect to track down.

He was able to access the suspect's rap sheet from his phone and had armed himself with that information before leaving the crime lab. Steve found his address of record, an apartment over a row of businesses in a building on 19th Avenue. He parked his vehicle across the street and paused to watch the building. He hesitated to text his team. First, he took a moment to try to work out logistics of making the arrest. Should he knock on the door and ask politely to speak with this guy, or kick it down and go in hard? He leaned toward the hard entry. One other thought occurred to him. He glanced at vehicles parked on the street, and wondered aloud, "OK, what kind of car would a drug dealer drive?" Something fancy, clean, taken care of, with a shiny exterior and power under the hood. In two separate areas, he found a couple of possibilities, a black Lexus and white Chrysler 300.

A door at the front of the building opened, and a tall muscular black man stepped out. Steve quickly glanced at his phone and scrolled to the mug shot on the rap sheet. From a distance, Steve confirmed it was the same guy. The suspect walked up to the Chrysler 300, and Steve silently congratulated himself on his powers of deduction. When the Chrysler started up, Steve pulled out into traffic behind him.

The drive was short. The Chrysler pulled to the side of the road on Stanyan Street, just outside the McDonald's. Steve drove past him, then quickly turned into the parking lot of a supermarket on Haight Street just across from the east end of Golden Gate Park. Green Resolve was just a couple blocks away. The suspect stayed in his car. He didn't feed the meter next to his car, but it appeared he might just be settling in.

Within two minutes, the suspect's first customer arrived. A young black man with short dreadlocks and sagging pants walked up the sidewalk. He stopped at the Chrysler and leaned down to the passenger window. Steve had a hard time seeing, but he knew what was going on. In one minute, having bought his weed, the customer walked away back the way he'd come.

He finally texted Scot. Knowing his message probably sounded cryptic, he set up a meeting point, without yet disclosing why.

It took the team twenty minutes to reach their meeting point. Steve had parked in the small parking lot outside the market. He soon spotted their black unmarked department issued Ford Explorer. As they approached, the team could see his attention was oriented across the street at the park.

As they got out, Scot walked up to the driver's window of Blazer's dark SUV. "Who are we watching?"

"Just down the street," Steve said. "See that white Chrysler 300?" He gave his men a moment to fix on the car. "CSI came back with a print on the crowbar," he continued. "Lynell Richards. Known dealer. I've dealt with him before." He handed Black his phone, and Scot scrolled through Richards' rap sheet.

"I thought our burglars wore gloves," Dave brought up.

"Yeah, they did. My theory is, he handled the bar without gloves before the burglary. If we bust him now, his lawyer may be able to poke holes in the bust because of that. But if he's holding contraband from the burglary, we might have a better case. Even if we don't, we can at least clear the burg and get some now-illicit weed off the street."

"And if he's not holding?" Scot asked.

Steve smiled. "I've seen a steady stream of people walking up to his car. Ten minutes ago, I followed him back to Green Resolve, where he shopped for five minutes, and returned here. Apparently, he had to restock his supply."

Scot nodded. "Yeah, he's holding."

A.J. shook his head. "His customers must not want to pay city taxes on store bought weed."

"Yet another argument against legalization," Steve agreed. "Dave, A.J., you guys see if you can position yourself behind him somewhere and maybe we can box him in."

Black handed Miano the keys to the Ford, and he hurried around to Blazer's passenger side. The unmarked drifted away, and Steve watched them pull out the exit and down Stanyan a block. A.J. was able to make a U-turn. Steve saw him pull the SUV to the side of the road just a few car lengths behind where the Chrysler was parked.

Steve picked up a small pair of binoculars from the center console. He lensed the Chrysler, watching intently for a moment. "He's not watching his surroundings at all, never saw the unmarked. Jeez, he's doing it right there in the open." Scot stayed silent, knowing his partner would explain. "You see his body language? How he's hunched over, his attention dedicated to something in his lap? His shoulders are moving, but only slightly. He's rolling a blunt right there in the car."

Scot said nothing, just gave his head a slight shake. They lapsed into silence for a moment.

Steve perked up when he saw two subjects approaching the vehicle. Two men, boys, really. Scrutinizing them, they couldn't have been more than sixteen or seventeen. One carried a small red backpack.

But something struck him, something he couldn't put his finger on. They seemed familiar, and he searched his memory…

He suddenly grabbed the push-to-talk radio from his center console and hit the transmit button. "We're moving in now. We're busting these two kids." He remembered where he'd seen these two, buying weed yesterday morning from the guy who came out of the Green Resolve. Lynell Richards was that guy. "Pull up alongside of them in the lane and I'll close off the front."

"Ten-four, we're ready to move," A.J. responded.

Steve started his vehicle and headed for the nearby driveway. For a minute, he divided his attention between tracking where the unmarked SUV was and making sure the boys did not leave just yet.

Steve pulled out of the parking lot, monitoring the other vehicle. He had to time the intercept just right.

* * *

Kevin and Randy walked along the edge of the park. "Are you sure about this guy?" Kevin asked, more from an unconscious desire for conversation than any kind of doubt about their destination.

"You met him yesterday," Shepherd replied. "He had good stuff then. He always has good stuff. What are you so worried about?"

Kevin let the retort go. "It was good stuff. I can practically taste that next blunt."

Randy spotted the dealer's Chrysler 300 parked just outside the McD's. "There," he muttered quietly. He scanned traffic quickly and darted into the street to cross. They boldly approached the Chrysler on the passenger side.

"Lynell, my man," Randy announced as they approached. "What's up? Got any trees?"

"Green for the green," Richards said, barely looking up from the blunt he was carefully rolling.

Having bought from Richards before, Randy leaned in the passenger window, reached across the passenger seat with a palmed bill. Richards still barely glanced up from his project, but he grasped Shepherd's hand, dragging the bill from it. He reached into a bag in his back seat, and handed up two small baggies, each with a single Cannabis bud.

Randy did not even glance up when a dark SUV rolled up next to the Chrysler, but Kevin did, and saw the vehicle stop suddenly. Another black SUV suddenly darted across the oncoming lane, lurching to a stop at an angle in the street, blocking the Chrysler in. The vehicles screamed cop.

He tapped Randy with the back of his hand and suddenly ran.

* * *

Steve steered left across the northbound lane and hit the brakes, blocking the vehicle in. A.J. stopped the unmarked next to the Chrysler, sealing the suspect vehicle from any immediate escape. Steve noted the red and blue light module on the dash now blinking.

Blazer was out of his car as soon as he stopped. "Police," he announced, "Everyone freeze."

No one froze. One of the boys suddenly took off running. Scot took off after him, skirting the unmarked and leaping onto the sidewalk. The second boy turned and tried to run after his friend. However, Steve was able to grab a handful of his backpack, and drag him back, practically off his feet. As he dragged the boy back, he paused for just a second, and confirmed that Dave had Richards covered. Castillo had burst from the SUV and in only a second had stuck his gun in the open driver window. The barrel pressed into Richards's neck. "Police," he said, "Put your hands on the wheel."

Steve dragged Randy away from the Chrysler, turned and threw the boy against the hood of his SUV. He held him there, again monitoring his teammates.

A.J. had stepped out the driver's side and skirted the front of their vehicle, approaching Dave's left. "Got him covered."

Dave holstered to have both hands free and opened driver's door. "Would you look at all that mari-ju-wanna," he commented, seeing the bag on the back seat.

Steve smirked when he heard this, remembering Lieutenant Cameron's joke.

"Step out of the car," Dave ordered.

As Richards climbed out, Dave felt him tense up. Dave tried to quickly set his stance, ready for the suspect to attack. As Richards reached his full height of six foot two, Dave found the man towering over him by a few inches. But he was ready when Richards used his bulk to try and shove past the cop. Dave body blocked him, shoving him back until he hit the corner of the open Chrysler door. Richards's back tensed from the shock of the pain. Dave grabbed his tensed arm and swung him around, propelling him into the side of the Chrysler. Dave pounced, his right hand holding Richards's arm against the back door, and his left pressing face to metal. "Are we done?" he asked.

The scene calmed for a moment, and Steve glanced around at his men. He then looked over at Scot, pursuing the last suspect.

* * *

Scot's feet pounded the sidewalk, his legs pumping faster trying to catch up with this kid. He was fast, but not too fast. "Police!" he called out, "You better stop!" Scot put on a burst of speed. In the back of his mind, he knew he was alone pursuing this kid. Blazer and the others had their hands full back in the parking lot. This being the case, he did not want the pursuit to get too far from their location. He closed the distance. He finally reached out and grabbed a shoulder, wrenching it back and knocking the kid off balance. He stumbled and Scot finally caught him. He grabbed hold of the kid's collar, pulling him to a stop. He reached with his left to secure an arm.

Despite being off balance, the kid tensed his body and suddenly threw a left elbow toward where he perceived the cop to be. Scot was ready when the body tensed, and he simply pivoted his arm up to block the flying elbow. He then grabbed the boy's wrist and pulled back, yanking him off balance and driving him backward to the ground. He pulled again, this time rolling the kid over for handcuffing.

* * *

Back at the scene of the bust, Steve watched Scot carefully as they grew further away, until Black brought the runner down. There was a bit of relief that his man was OK, not that he couldn't take care of himself. He allowed himself a dry smile as Scot walked their runner back to the group. Scot tossed Blazer the kid's wallet and directed him to, "Sit down."

Kevin sat down next to Randy on a curb. The cops stood over them, and to the boys, the cops looked like they were just trying to appear menacing. They didn't pull it off.

Steve stepped up to where Dave was patting down a handcuffed Lynell. Dave motioned to the car. Steve glanced inside. The forgotten blunt sat on the console. He leaned in and used a single finger to pull open the gym bag on the back seat. It had a small pile of baggies of bud. "Lynell," he clucked, "That looks like a little more than personal use."

Lynell said nothing, but one of the kids on the curb piped up. "It's an infraction, cop. Simple fine. Why are you wasting your time on a little bit of weed?"

Steve picked up the kid's wallet and dug around inside. "How old are you...Randy?"

The kid hesitated for just a moment. "Twenty."

"That's not what your fake ID says." He found the obvious fake hidden in the same wallet pouch as the real one. The bright ones made his job so much easier. "I bet if we run you through the system, we find out you're underage."

"You're gonna do all that for just a little weed?" Randy said. "You like wasting your time? The stuff's practically legal."

"Kid, let me clue you in on something. You have a long life ahead of you. This is one of those situations that you can learn from. This is one of those situations," and he made exaggerated air quotes with his fingers, "where 'legal' does not translate to 'good idea'. This is California, we have a lot of those. Pot is not legal until January." He gestured at Lynell. "Ordinarily, your friend from Green Resolve here would probably get a small fine and be back on the streets slinging his dope by tonight. He's actually got a whole other problem he's going to have to deal with." Lynell's face darkened when he heard this. "But you, my friend. You're underage. This stuff that is so "practically legal" is not legal to you for I'd say another four years. You guys completed your transaction here, therefore, you're going into the system." To Scot, he said, "Let's get a black and white out here and transport them to Mission Rock."

Scot caught Steve's eye and nodded him aside. When Steve had joined him by the SUV, Scot said, "You sure you want to do this? It is just for some weed."

"And?" Steve said, his eyes turning dark and cold on his partner. "What, you want to just let them go? That's not going to do them any favors. I know how this is going to go. Lynell goes in for the burglary which some DA may or may not reduce through Prop 47. But these two get booked into the juvenile system, we call their parents, call *their* attention to the problem, they get a court date, and maybe get into a diversion program. If they divert from this shit, great, the police saved their lives. If not, we'll be picking up their dead pieces someday."

Scot shook his head. "We can always call their parents from here."

"You think they'll give you phone numbers? No, the parents can come pick them up at the station." He glanced over at A.J., who was on his cell phone, and nodded—a patrol unit was en route.

* * *

The entire group returned to Mission Rock, the police headquarters on 3rd Street. Steve sent Miano and Castillo to their basement office with the boys with instructions to book them and call their parents. They would be held until parents arrived to pick them up. He and Scot took Lynell up to the Homicide squad room, where they secured him in an interview room. Scot stood by to watch the suspect through the observation window while Steve went to brief Captain Stanson. When Blazer returned minutes later he joined Scot briefly in the observation room.

"He looks awfully confused," Scot muttered.

"We should go enlighten him."

They stepped outside, around the corner and into the interview room. Steve noted a change on Lynell's face that amused him. He went from looking incredulous to smug. "Man, I don't know what you cops think you got me here for, busting me for some damn weed."

Steve smiled as he sat down opposite the dealer. "You've been advised of your rights, correct? You don't want your lawyer here?"

"I don't need a damn lawyer, 'cause y'all ain't got shit on me!"

"You're right, Lynell," Steve said, still smiling. "Marijuana has been decriminalized. Ordinarily, for having some weed, we're talking a ticket and fine. Of course, we could talk to you about toking up in public, which is not legal."

"Actually," Scot spoke up, "he never got to light that blunt. We got there too quick."

"You are absolutely right, Inspector," Steve said. "We can't get you on that. We could talk about the amount of weed you had, which exceeds the amount considered for personal use. Then again, DAs don't take that seriously either." Steve leaned back, his own face growing noticeably smug. "We could talk about Green Resolve. We could talk about how you buy discounted weed there and sell it on the streets, even right behind their building. Oh, and how you sell it to juveniles like those two clowns we busted you with. Hell, that's enough to get that dispensary shut down." Steve leaned in again. "We can talk about the weed you had in your car. Like where you got it. Did you even bother to change the packaging? We happen to know it came from that dispensary burglary on 16th Street. We know you did that break-in. We've got your fingerprint on the crowbar you tossed in the corner." He paused. "Which of these topics would you like to discuss?"

He could see the wheels turning in Lynell's mind. The dealer finally smirked. "I'll take that lawyer now."

Steve smirked right back at him. He rose, and Scot preceded him out the door. Steve paused before leaving. "I can't decide if that is the dumbest move you've made, the smartest…or if it even makes a difference."

Outside, Steve took a couple of deep breaths to calm down. Scot had started to walk away but turned back when he saw Steve was not behind him.

He saw how distressed Blazer was. He really did take this shit seriously. Scot took a step back to his boss, but paused, not really knowing what to say.

Steve felt his cell phone vibrate, and he whipped it from his belt. "Blazer."

"It's Cameron. We checked out a few more potential grow houses. We found one you might want to take a look at."

"Text me the address." When he hung up, he said to Scot, "Vice may have another grow house. Lynell can remain in detention for the time being. We'll get the case ready for the DA later." When his phone beeped again, he glanced at the screen, then tapped it. "I'm texting Castillo the address, they can meet us there. Let's go."

* * *

As they left the station, Steve noted the clouds that punctuated the gathering late afternoon darkness. This was not a simple fog bank. The weather report had earlier said that more rain was coming. After a long hot summer, even by San Francisco standards, and sparse storms during the fall, a good soaking rain would do this dirty city good.

In twenty minutes, Steve pulled to the edge of the road on a block of Victorians in the south east corner of the Mission District, just blocks from San Francisco General Hospital. The address that Cameron had texted him was a house located in the center of the row of Victorians. Cameron's unmarked vehicle was parked a few spaces ahead. The Lieutenant saw Blazer's black SUV pull to the curb and got out to contact the Special Forces Sergeant.

"This is only the second place we've checked," Cameron said as he stepped up to the driver window of Steve's black SUV. "We got a look at the power setup in back." He held up his cell phone to show Blazer the pics he'd taken. Steve glanced over the photo, showing a mass of twisted wires that was all jumbled together. He scrolled through a quick series on the phone.

"Looks like this could be a deathtrap."

"We've been watching the place for a bit. No traffic, no one in or out."

"I'll call Judge Allen." Steve pulled out his own cell. After the previous bust, he now had the Judge on speed dial. "Judge Allen, it's Sergeant Steve Blazer, SFPD."

"Good afternoon, Sergeant."

"Sir, I hate to bug you this late in the afternoon, but I'm looking at another likely drug distribution house, and I'd like to get a telephone warrant to make a bust."

"I heard that the last bust resulted in a large illegal marijuana grow," Allen said, his voice completely neutral. "Is this another one?"

The tone of voice gave Steve pause. He'd been purposely vague before. Was this Judge on the side of the weed industry? Was Steve about to lose his conduit into shutting down the illegal weed trade. "Yes, sir, it is another possible marijuana grow."

The Judge's answer surprised him. "Good. You know, my wife and I used to own some land out in the East Bay. We rented it to this young couple, they seemed nice enough, until I found out they turned the house into a marijuana grow. They turned out to be horrible people, started a fire with their drug activity, nearly burned the house down. They got raided by the California Bureau of Narcotics Enforcement. They ended up seizing the property and I had a legal battle on my hands. This legalization is going to cause too many problems, but in the meantime...I'm glad someone is having the balls to shut down the illegal dealers. I'm authorizing you to search this house."

Steve had a growing smile as the Judge laid out the details of the telephone warrant. "Yes, sir, and thank you very much." He tapped his phone screen, ending the call. "We got it."

Cameron turned from the driver window and signaled the officers in his own unmarked SUV.

As the Lieutenant walked away, Steve said to Scot, "Wait 'till I tell you the story the Judge just told me."

Special Forces gathered at the back of Steve's SUV, and everyone donned their tactical vests, which were loaded down with magazines for their sidearms. Steve watched the house carefully as he prepared his equipment. He went over his options on how to make entry. When Cameron joined him with his men, Steve said, "You think no one's home?"

"We haven't seen any movement."

Steve eyed the heavy metal battering ram that Inspector Chandler from Vice carried. "Then I think we can forego tactical approach. I think I'll start by knocking on the door." Without waiting for a response, he started for the front door. With several of the officers from Vice and Special Forces sharing a collective shrug, they trooped after him.

Raindrops began to pelt them as they quietly climbed the steps. The sun was dropping behind the horizon, shielded by the rain clouds and giving the twilight an eerie shade of gray. Steve eyed each window, but all were covered by tin foil. The cops lined up on one side of the door. Steve saw that Chandler had brought the battering ram just in case. When everyone was set, he pounded on the door. "San Francisco Police, we have a search warrant!" he shouted.

His shout faded to silence. There was no movement or noise from inside.

Steve shrugged and nodded Chandler up to the door.

Inspector Chandler was tall and solidly built, with an angular face accented by a dark goatee. He hefted the steel battering ram, stepped up to the door and gave it a casual swing. The flat end impacted just next to the doorknob. The latch was torn away and the door swung inward.

They filed in, guns drawn, and fanned out. Steve's initial glance over the interior of the house confirmed what they had suspected. The home was turned into a greenhouse, with marijuana plants lining every room. Once he confirmed the plants, he concentrated on the safety of his men. They checked every room, every closet, every place large enough to hide a human being. In one minute, the house was singing with shouts of, "Clear!"

Steve made his way to the back, exploring further. He found a back door and looked outside. He saw shaded gardens outside, now dripping with the rain. He stepped out onto a rickety deck with stairs leading down to a kind of community garden. He sought out the electrical box that Cameron had photographed and found it just off the edge of the deck, near the back corner, and next to the house that abutted it next door. In the diminishing light, he checked that box, briefly, confirming what Cameron had found. He then turned back to the door and went inside.

He didn't see that the rain had started running off the roof onto the jumble of wires that protruded from the panel. He didn't see the arc that suddenly lit the deck.

Steve rejoined his team inside. "Let's get an evidence team out here," he suggested to Cameron, "but I'd like to get some initial photographs of everything. Maybe get a count of how many plants we have." He turned to Scot, "See if you can find any papers or documentation stashed somewhere. Maybe we can find an owner and question him." Scot nodded and moved off on his search.

A.J. examined the environmental set-up. He looked up and caught Steve's eye. "It's crude, but it gets the job done. They've got heat lamps arranged in every room, what looks like one for every plant. They have a timed watering system that basically leaches water into each bucket at certain hours. They also have a mister set up in every room."

"It does feel kind of humid in here," Steve commented. "That's the kind of thing that can warp walls." He stepped around the end of the row of plants and felt something under foot. He glanced at the floor, and saw what he had stepped on, an orange electrical extension cord. These cords ran everywhere through the house he soon saw, plugging into every outlet and in many cases multiple plug strips per outlet.

Scot found Blazer. "I've checked every room, kitchen, bedrooms. I can't find any papers here. Obviously, nobody actually lives here."

Steve nodded. Cameron returned, having retrieved a digital camera from his vehicle. Starting in the front room, he began taking pictures of the tables and shelving units with buckets and planters, and marijuana plants of varying sizes.

Steve took a moment to walk upstairs, eyeing the electrical cords that snaked up to the second floor. The cords were loose, not banded together to prevent tripping.

The second floor felt cramped and closed in, three bedrooms, none used for sleeping. He found more of the same, tables and shelves with marijuana plants. The plants here appeared smaller, younger in their growth stage. The electrical cord hazard was prevalent here as well.

As he started down the stairs, he missed a flicker of light from a back window that overlooked the garden.

He traipsed downstairs, careful to avoid the electrical cords. The rest of the teams had formed in the front room, where Cameron was taking pictures.

"Does anyone else smell smoke?" Scot suddenly asked.

The group fell silent as the odor registered. Steve saw the haze, and immediately ducked through the kitchen to the back door. He recoiled when he saw the back corner of the house ablaze.

His men entered the room and immediately threw arms over their faces to shield from the heat. Scot ducked back out of the room. He'd seen a small fire extinguisher in the kitchen and raced to retrieve it. In the seconds that he was gone, the flames seemed to grow. The blaze licked up the outside of the house, unabated by the light rain. They had eaten through the wall to the interior, and now consumed the entire wall, flames chasing the smoke pouring onto the ceiling.

Scot ran back in, pushed through his teammates, and attacked the fire with the extinguisher. He saw immediately that it would be useless, but he kept spraying at the base of where the flames ate the wall.

Only seconds into the attack, Steve called out, "Forget it, losing battle." He coughed once and shouted, "Let's get out of here."

Smoke was now pouring from the back room, beginning to fill the house. The odor of marijuana smoke reached them as plants in the back room were now consumed. "Outside!" Steve called, posting by the door to make sure all of his men escaped and were accounted for.

"Should we try to grab a few of these plants?" Cameron asked as he paused by the door.

"Hell, no," Steve said, "Let them burn with the house."

Once everyone had exited, Blazer and Cameron made themselves the last to leave. Steve reached the street, drawing fresh air into his lungs. The marijuana smoke stench was still prevalent, in his clothes now, he realized. He glanced at Cameron, and they looked back at the house. "Let the stoner block party begin," Steve muttered.

He found that his men were rushing to other houses in the row, banging on doors to evacuate residents. "I suppose one of us should call the fire department," Steve said facetiously, and fished out his cell phone.

* * *

The fire department arrived in minutes. By that time, smoke was pouring out the open front door, and the flames had reached the second floor. Residents from other homes surrounding the Victorian were gathered in the streets. As the fire department set up to battle the flames, Steve directed his men to begin canvassing the neighbors. Did they know the neighbors that owned the house? Were they aware of the business of those neighbors? One minute after their arrival, the fire department began laying water on the flames. The Victorian was fully engulfed, but when Steve briefly conferred with the fire captain, he was told that their primary goal now was to keep the flames from spreading to the neighboring homes. By now the odor of the smoke was prevalent, and anyone who knew the odor of marijuana knew that smell. Steve sent out a text to his men, inquiring whether they'd had any luck. The texts he received back all said the same thing. The neighbors had never met this homeowner and had no clue the house was being used in such a manner.

Steve and Cameron maintained a post near the fire department's command vehicle. They would confer from time to time as they watched the progress of the fire department, but gradually, Steve fell silent, contemplating his next move.

"What the hell happened here?" a high-pitched male voice suddenly screamed nearby. Steve glanced over, seeing a bearded man in his early forties staring at the smoking ruins of the Victorian. He was short, maybe five-eight, but his hairy arms gestured in a big way. "What the hell's going on here?"

Steve approached him. "Sir, are you the owner of the house?"

"Yes, that's my house! What the hell—?"

"I'm Sergeant Blazer, SFPD, can I ask your name?"

"My name is Noah Seberg."

"Mr. Seberg, do you live in the house?"

"No, I have an apartment a few blocks from here. I was on my way home and saw the fire trucks. What—?"

"Sir, are you aware of the large marijuana grow inside the house?"

"Yes! I grow medical cannabis for several of the nearby dispensaries. I'm licensed and everything. This is a legal operation." He seemed to see Blazer's badge for the first time. "What happened, did you cops try to bust a legal grow? Who's responsible for *this*?"

Steve gave him a blank stare. "You are."

Seberg gave him a confused look.

"Who does your electrical, Mr. Seberg?" Steve turned to Cameron, who handed over his cell phone. Steve showed him Seberg the picture of the jumbled wires at the electrical box. "This is what we found at the back of your grow house. All those special heating systems and watering systems, cords running everywhere, special modifications to that box. Are you insured for all that marijuana? There's going to be a thorough investigation of this fire. I bet your insurance company will be very interested in the cause of all this."

During the speech, Seberg had slowly deflated, starting the moment he saw the picture. When Steve finished, he huffed once, then took a minute to build himself up again. "We'll see." He fished out a cell phone and stepped away.

Steve returned the Lieutenant's cell phone. "That was fun," he smiled.

* * *

They spent the next several hours, well into the evening, working the fire scene. Once the fire was put out and they were let back in, Steve got a detailed look at the damage. The interior was a total loss. Plastic watering pipes lay in melted ruins. Many of the tables and shelves had collapsed. Steve noted with some satisfaction that, in every room, all plants were ruined, either wilted beyond repair or charred completely. Pieces of the charred electrical box were collected as evidence—they were careful to preserve this, since Steve knew that Seberg would likely try to state that the police had been responsible for the fire. Cameron already had pictures of the chaotic wiring, as well as the electrical cords everywhere and the plants at various stages. Steve and Cameron discussed loading the plants and other evidence into a vehicle for removal and destruction.

With all this, they managed to wrap up the crime scene around seven pm. Blazer and Cameron excused their men for the night, and they departed from the scene to go home. However, Steve then received an urgent text from Captain Stanson: My office, ASAP!

Blazer strolled into the Captain's office just before seven-thirty. He was greeted by another face, a short man in a suit, about his age, with short thinning curly hair.

"Sergeant Blazer, meet Assistant District Attorney Kline," Stanson said. Kline did not offer a handshake, so Blazer did not either.

"Are you here about the Lynell Richards case?" Steve asked. "I just turned that in about four hours ago."

"Lynell Richards?" Kline asked. "That was a non-violent burg."

Steve's eyebrows hit the ceiling. He was suddenly not optimistic about where this discussion was going. "You're going to prop 47 him? We got him dead to rights. Then again, the burg was just a pot shop. Maybe that's justice."

Kline turned even more smug. "Actually, Sergeant, I am here about the cannabis industry in general. I've received the files on the grow houses you busted yesterday."

"Good?" Steve said. He feared where this was going.

"Including the one you took down just today. The one that turned out to be a legal growing operation. The one that burned down."

"I think you'll see with the evidence we have, that fire was caused by the owner's negligence. We see this all the time, counselor, someone tries to rewire their power circuits, or steal power, or just plain overloads their facility with all the shit they're running…it's a huge hazard, and it leads to the dangers we've seen the last two days."

"Sergeant, that legit business owner has my personal cell number. He's advised me that he plans to sue the department and the city for the destruction of his property."

Steve shrugged. "Stand up to him. Fight him in court. You're going to have an airtight case. Arson investigators are at the scene now, and they will reach the same conclusion. We didn't cause that fire, him messing with the electrical did."

"You don't get it, Sergeant. Cannabis has become a big business in this city."

Steve rolled his eyes. "I'm aware."

"He's going to create so much negative publicity for this department, the entire city will turn against the police."

"Someone beat him to it. That's already happened. I'm a cop, I live with that every day."

"And all because you had to go after a harmless drug that is about to be legal."

Steve face became ice, as the fire in his eyes grew. "Counselor, I get that cannabis is about to be legal in this state. For years, there has been a steady stream of propaganda from the other side to minimize the stigma of potheads. In 2016, enough people finally decided that pot was harmless and decided to legalize for recreational use. Yes, I said propaganda. Because those behind the campaign didn't show the other side of marijuana use. They don't show the broken families, kids failing in schools, issues with physical and mental health. There are lots of people who want nothing to do with this drug, and those same people will have no recourse when this drug becomes legal. There are so many questions that haven't been answered, like what happens when businesses have to fire someone who causes harm while on the job? What about all the DUI issues cops are finding? Even worse, what about the DUI accidents we *will* see? What about the gateway effect, counselor? The gateway effect is very real. Some of the kids I've dealt with on the streets, I've watched them graduate from weed, to coke to meth. There's a whole other side to this issue that the public doesn't see. This harmless drug is more harmful than anyone realizes."

Kline had become more and more uncomfortable as the speech went on. As Steve's speech wound down, he let the silence linger on too long. "Look, Sergeant, no one cares about a little weed anymore."

"You see what you just did there?" Steve said. "A little weed. You minimized the problem. That kind of thinking causes one to turn a blind eye to the bigger issues."

"You're missing the point. Police departments all over the country, including this one by the way, have started taking a hands-off approach to marijuana."

"To everyone's peril," Steve interjected.

"It's a losing battle."

"I want to make something perfectly clear to you, Counselor," Steve said firmly. "Look around you on your drive home today. Watch the news tonight. Do you think society is getting better because of this drug? The more we lose this battle, the more we have to clean up after it."

"Mr. Kline, thank you for coming by," Stanson stepped in. "We'll see that you get an airtight case regarding this fire. We want you on solid ground when you do go to court if this guy does decide to sue."

Kline was deflated by the interruption. He glanced at Stanson, then turned a hard glare at Blazer. He couldn't think of any last words to say, so he stalked out of the office.

Once the door was closed, Steve said, "This guy looks like an actual weasel."

"Did you catch what he said?" Stanson brought up. "This guy, what's his name, Seberg? He has Kline's personal cell. I think Kline may have been a part of the legalization campaign."

"More good news," Steve retorted.

"Put him at the back of your mind, but he will pop up again. Go home, sleep on this. Tomorrow, let's look at this issue with fresh eyes."

Steve saw the wisdom in this. He nodded and left.

* * *

Kevin Donner had to wait until nearly seven p.m. before he could be picked up from the Mission Rock Police station where he was detained. His mom was working overtime at the diner, so he was forced to call his dad. There was a delay in the pigs processing him, and once he was offered his phone calls, he hesitated for a while before calling home. He waited patiently in a chair outside the processing area, handcuffed to a bench. He finally saw a uniformed officer lead his father into the room. Dad didn't say anything as the officer uncuffed the boy. They were escorted out to the front door. Dad waited until they were halfway to the truck before he said anything. When he did speak, it was with a hand slapping across the back of Kevin's head.

Startled, the boy ducked away the slap with a faint cry of surprise.

"What the hell's wrong with you, boy?" his dad yelled.

"What?" Kevin said, glancing around for any witnesses. "What's the big deal?"

"What's the big deal? You called me from the police station. Cops just told me you were grabbed up in a drug bust."

"It wasn't a drug bust. This guy from school just had some weed."

"That's a drug bust, you little shit." The insult stung, and Kevin saw the look of guilt on his dad's face. He'd taken the anger too far and took a breath to calm down. "You're supposed to be grounded, Kevin."

"Why? What did I do?"

"The way you've been acting, this has been a long time coming. You will go nowhere except school and home."

"But I have a party to go to tonight!"

"Not anymore. Not for a while. Your behavior has been unacceptable lately. That shit stops now. We're going home, you're doing homework and going straight to bed. Get in the car." They'd reached Dad's ancient 70s model Ford pickup. He may be on disability from his previous job, but he did know engines, and he'd been able to keep this beast running long past its life span. They had paused outside so Dad could continue his lecture. Kevin now wrenched open the door and climbed inside.

As Dad walked around the other side, Kevin fumed and avoided his gaze. He stared at the police headquarters building, which had come to symbolize everything he hated in life. There was no way he was missing this party tonight. He began to plot his escape.

CHAPTER 5

In his last little while on duty that day, Steve traded a few texts with his girlfriend, Susan Wolf. She was on patrol, but her shift was wrapping up. Steve hung out alone in the Special Forces Squad Room, waiting for her to finish her shift. One final text received from her stated that she was done and waiting for him in the parking lot. They met up and she followed him in her car toward his apartment. There was an excess of vehicles parked on Steve's block and they were lucky to find parking on the street, although not directly in front of the building. Suzy parked her Nissan Titan a few spaces from his SUV. Carrying their black patrol bags, they padded down a slight hill toward his building.

Steve sensed something wrong as they reached the front doorway. Above him, on the third floor, he could hear music and voices coming from an open window.

Suzy heard it and sensed a potential problem as well. "New neighbors?"

"They've been there about three months, a couple of college guys. I guess they're throwing a pre-New Year party. I guess this is why there are so many cars here."

As they mounted the steps up to the stoop, the front door to the building opened. An elderly couple stepped carefully outside. When she saw him, the woman called out, "Steven, thank goodness you're here."

"Good evening, Vera, Albert. What's the trouble?" Steve asked, knowing the answer.

"It's that Simon fellow on three. They've been throwing parties every night this week. Right now, he has guests out in the hallway, and they're smoking that awful marijuana. We live above both of you, and even from two floors away, that awful smoke gets into our apartment. Can't something be done?"

Suzy glanced at Steve, knowing this was the battle he'd been fighting all week. Steve lived on the fourth floor, so this charming couple must live right above him.

"Have you guys tried calling the Super?" Steve asked.

"Malik?" Albert said. "I called him this afternoon, but I think he was already drunk for the night."

Steve huffed. Their building Superintendent was pretty useless, a lazy bum who seemed to live his life in an alcoholic haze.

He glanced up at the open window. "Let me go talk to Simon. Maybe I can at least get him to keep his guests inside."

The offer was not meant to be evasive, and he certainly knew that his doing this bare minimum would not be enough to keep the marijuana smoke from continuing to drift upstairs. but his offer still had the effect of at least reassuring his neighbor that something would be done. "Bless you, Steven. It is good to have a policeman living here." Albert said nothing but did offer a handshake and a smile.

Steve led the way inside. There was no elevator

and he and Suzy started up a carpeted staircase.

"We're probably not going to be able to do much," Suzy said.

"Oh, there's plenty I can do," Steve growled. He stifled his anger for a moment. "I'm just sorry it's cutting into our off time together."

"Don't worry about me. I'm right behind you." She smiled and added, "Steven."

Even before they reached the third floor, Steve could smell the odor of marijuana smoke. When he reached the third-floor landing, they found a group of four young white men lounging and talking there. Two of them were side by side, sitting on the stairs, blocking the pathway. They were sharing a blunt. "Excuse me, guys," Steve said, perfectly polite.

The pair did not move. After a three second pause, one finally looked up at him. "Guys, this ain't a bench. If one of those blunts catches the building on fire, people are going to want to get out, and you're blocking their escape. You need to move."

There was more hesitation, but the pair did finally get up. They retreated to the wall and resumed puffing their blunt.

Steve gave Suzy his patrol bag, and she mounted the staircase briefly to toss the bags up onto the next landing. She wanted to be able to watch Steve and back him up if necessary.

Steve stopped at the front door, which was wide open. Legally, he could not yet enter someone else's dwelling, so he stopped to at least survey the interior. He saw at least a dozen people, mostly men, with a couple of girls. They were lounging on any horizontal surface, some watching a TV in the corner. He saw a few containers of alcohol but weed seemed to be the drug of choice. Everyone seemed to be smoking some.

"Hey, cutey," a smile greeted him. A young girl,

maybe not even twenty had sidled up to the door. "When did you get here?"

Steve dug up a half smile. "How's it going? I'm looking for Simon."

"I think he's in the kitchen. Come on in."

Consent granted, Steve thought, at least for now. Need to use it while I have it. He stepped inside, scoping every face for the one belonging to his neighbor. He spotted the familiar face as Simon stepped from his kitchen. Steve skirted a couch loaded with party guests and approached his neighbor.

Simon was young, looked to be about twenty. He had the physique of a college age surfer, and right now wore the shorts and Hawaiian shirt to support the stereotype. His blond hair was just a shade lighter than Blazer's sandy high-and-tight.

Just as Steve was about to make contact, one of the guests rushed across the room. He was shaking a baggie and held it up to provide a good view to his host—and Blazer. "Dude, you gotta try this Kush. This shit will free your mind."

Simon's eyes went from the bag to his neighbor, and they suddenly went wide.

He never got a chance to speak with Blazer. His buddy grabbed his shoulders. "Dude, New Year's Day, just a few more days, and this stuff is free and clear, we can smoke as much as we want, wherever we want."

Simon finally got a chance to confront his neighbor. "Steve, right?"

Steve was seething at what Kush-boy had just said, knowing how untrue it was supposed to be. "Simon, we got a problem," he said. "All your guests smoking up the hallway ain't cool."

"Who the hell are you?" Kush-boy said.

Steve ignored him for the moment. "You've got neighbors, including myself, who don't appreciate the smell of weed. It would be great if you could at least have some respect for your neighbors—"

"Hey, pal, maybe you should tell those neighbors to get with the times. If they don't like a little smoke, they can personally kiss my ass."

"Dude, shut up," Simon begged his friend.

"No, dude, I got this." Kush-boy was on a roll. "Why don't you produce these alleged problem neighbors. I'd like to laugh in their faces."

Steve finally turned to Kush-boy. "Do you have any respect for anyone?"

"Respect is overrated, dude."

Steve let a hint of a smile tug at his lips. "I bet I can shut down that attitude of yours."

Kush-boy laughed. "What are you going to do, big man?"

Steve pulled at the chain around his neck, pulling his badge out from under his shirt. Kush-boy's eyes quickly went wide. He turned and disappeared.

"Steve, I'm sorry," Simon said. "I tried to tell him you're a cop."

"Here's how this is going to play out," Steve said. "This party is over. If I still smell this shit in thirty minutes, I get a black-and-white out here, and we ticket every car on this block. If my buddy officers detect any pot smell on anyone, or catch someone holding, or smoking a joint...we'll find out just how legal the shit really is. Pass the word." Steve turned and walked to the door.

Simon tried to follow, calling out over and over to his back, "I'm sorry! I'm sorry!"

Steve ignored him. Suzy was waiting for him in the hallway. With Simon, and a couple of his guests, staring at their backs, they went upstairs.

* * *

Kevin lay alone in his bed. When he and his dad arrived home, his mom had something resembling dinner waiting. Kevin had no desire to sit with them and be grilled about his run in with the cops. He had even less desire to sit there while his dad belittled him, and his mom tried feebly to minimize his misbehavior. Upon returning home, he simply stormed past his parents and locked himself in his room. For the first hour, he had found a rubber ball—he had no idea where he had acquired it—and threw it against the wall over and over, just to occupy his mind. Along the way, he heard his parents arguing again, so he slipped in his earbuds and blasted a post-punk playlist from his cell phone. When his digital clock radio said it was eleven o'clock, he yanked out his earbuds.

The house was finally quiet. Both his parents had probably drunk themselves to unconsciousness, and most likely in separate rooms. It was the same as every other night.

Kevin didn't bother opening his door to check the living room and see if anyone was there and awake—what if he was wrong? He simply opened his window and climbed out. There was a gas pipeline and meter right outside his window that provided a convenient stepping stool. In moments, he was outside, heading across the yard and slipping quietly out the back gate. Once out of the alley and on the street, he fished out the cell phone and called Randy. They had a party to get to.

* * *

Steve led Suzy into his apartment. They both dropped their patrol bags by a stand near the door. They would be moved later. Without regard to his girlfriend, Steve walked straight to his stereo. He hit play on the CD player. A rousing rock anthem practically erupted from the speakers. Suzy had an appreciation for the classic rock that Steve loved, and she had seen how much he loved his music. At least now, he had the courtesy to turn the volume down a bit.

Looking at him across the room, she could see that he was seething.

"Don't let that guy get to you," she said.

Steve turned to her and took a breath to gather himself. "It's not just him. All day today, I've run into example after example of the attitude that is permeating our society now: 'Marijuana is no big deal.' 'It's practically legal.'"

"In a few days, it will be legal."

"I'm aware. I'm also aware of the problems that everyone wants to deny. You know the new law states that someone caught smoking in public will receive a hundred dollar fine? But are any of us cops going to enforce it? Will there be any weed citations handed out? These kids just go get their cards from someone with the bare minimum first aid training, and they think it gives them a license to do whatever they want. Meanwhile, more and more kids are getting turned on to the stuff. Because now, the attitude has changed. 'If the government says it's legal, it must not be harmful.'" He'd gotten himself worked up again and took a moment to calm down.

"There are kids out there right now getting introduced to it. The gateway effect in all its reality. I had an instructor in my academy—you probably had the same guy. He really believed in the gateway effect, as much as I do. The story goes, let's say you have someone who wants to get high. He's hanging out with his buddies, and he says to his buddies, 'you got any weed?' And his buddy says, 'No, but I got this other shit you should try.' That's how it starts."

* * *

Kevin wandered the crowded house. Some classmate had decided to live it up because his rich parents were out of town for the week. The party was in a Victorian several blocks from his own home. There had to be a hundred people here. The living room had a stereo system that blared tunes while people there danced. Someone had brought a keg of beer and someone else had swiped a couple bottles from a guardian's liquor cabinet. He and Randy had walked in without anyone greeting them at the door. They found a couch, complete with girls kissing on or grinding on random dudes at either end. Someone handed Kevin a cup of beer, and he chugged it without question. He sat on the couch, still fuming about his incident earlier that day.

After a few minutes, he discovered that Randy had left him. He tossed his empty cup aside and went to look for his buddy. He maneuvered himself between people, searching. He finally came across Randy sitting on a barstool in the kitchen. Across the counter, someone pushed a red plastic cup toward Randy.

Kevin approached. "What's up, Quinn?" he said to Randy's friend.

"What's up, Kevin?"

Donner turned to Randy. "Bro, I need something. You got any trees?"

"Sorry, dude, my forest is barren."

Kevin looked over at Quinn. "How about you? You got anything I can smoke?"

"Sorry, I'm all out of weed. But...I have something else I know you'd like." He pushed the cup he'd offered Randy toward Donner. Kevin looked into the cup and saw a little blue pill.

He almost stopped himself, but said, "What is it?"

"Only the second most popular thing to ever come out of Amsterdam. This shit will have you tripping through the stars. It will have you in," and he leaned in to put an enticing lilt on the word, "ecstasy."

Kevin kept a stone face. He hesitated all of one second, then grabbed the cup and tossed the single pill into his mouth. He found another cup of beer nearby and washed it down. This was accompanied by cheers from his two classmates and a slap on the back by Randy.

* * *

"For as long as I can until January first, and even beyond if I can, I will take as much of this illegal weed off the street as I can," Steve said. Suzy was sitting on his couch, and Steve returned from his kitchen with bottles of water. "It won't end up in the hands of some dealer to give to some kid who wants to try it."

"And these are not people who would be," she made air quotes, "'doing it anyway.'"

"Yes, another of the classic rationalizations used by the 'Legalize Now' crowd. This is the very definition of a "pusher." These guys push the shit on vulnerable people. If I can keep some dope out of the hands of a pusher, that vulnerable kid doesn't have his mind screwed with, and he has one more day to make better choices, instead of being enslaved by the drug."

Suzy suddenly leaned in and kissed him. At first it was an effort to get him to shut up about the marijuana issue to they could talk about more pleasurable topics and activities. But then she regretted her next question. With a flirty smile, she asked, "Have you done the walk of shame?"

Steve managed to grin back. "Not lately. You?"

She cocked her head. "A couple times, during my

heavy drinking days. Not lately?" she chided him. "You never snuck out on a girl after a one-night stand?"

"I faced it head on," he answered. "But I also never took advantage of someone in such a vulnerable state."

* * *

Kevin was flying high. The ecstasy plowed through his blood, bombarding his brain with sensations. He found his way to a conveniently empty couch and plopped into it. Someone opened a door nearby, and from the light inside that room, his senses were flooded with bright swirling lights. He smiled at the brilliant colors.

The door slammed, and the noise rumbled in his head as the colors wore down. He then got a look at new activity at the door. A girl's face swam into focus, and he struggled in his mind to remember her name...Jessica...Jessica Kline. She was pretty. He'd seen her around school, remembered her from before he started cutting so much. She was kind of short, too skinny to fill out a pair of jeans, but had a round face that was darkly beautiful, piercing blue eyes and straight blond hair. She was beautiful enough to have caught the eye of one of the school's football jocks, Lee Piker. Kevin was out of date on the campus gossip, but Lee and Jessica had been going out awhile, he didn't know how long. Kevin tilted his head to focus on Jessica. He wouldn't go so far as to say he had a crush on her, but he had always found her...interesting, but out of his league and out of reach. She always caught his eye when he passed her in the hallway. But the last couple weeks—before he started cutting school more frequently—she seemed troubled. Sad.

Seeing her slam the door, he suddenly got an eyeful as to why she was so troubled. Seconds later, the door was yanked open again. Piker stepped out and confronted her. "What is your problem?"

"My problem?" she screamed over the loud music. "You promised me you were not doing anything behind my back, and now I find you feeling up that... skank!"

"Jess, come on, it didn't mean anything. You know I love you—."

Jessica threw up her hands and turned to stalk off. Piker grabbed her arm, but she threw him off, took one step away, but turned back, knowing he was trying to follow her. As another kid tried to walk past, she stepped aside and suddenly shoved him full-force into her now ex-boyfriend. Piker tangled with the unsuspecting teen, and Jessica used the distraction to duck into a small group and disappear. Lee untangled himself from the other kid and shoved his way through the crowd to try and find her.

Seeing all this from just a few feet away, Kevin made a quick decision. He jumped up from his couch and followed them. Lee stopped outside the crowd, searching over them for any sign of Jessica. He didn't see her right away and he apparently gave up the search for the moment. Kevin saw him turn back toward the door he'd come out of, presumably to return to the skank he'd left there. He never noticed Kevin's interest in the situation.

Once Lee was gone, Kevin ran into the next room, searching for Jessica. He saw her pushing her way toward the front door. She had her best friend in tow, a girl he remembered as Elizabeth, who was urgently asking Jessica what was wrong.

He ran toward them. Jessica was reaching for the front door when he suddenly collided with the door right in front of her, surprising her and her friend.

"Don't go," he said.

She looked astonished but couldn't yet bring herself to say anything.

"Look, Lee's an ass, he doesn't deserve you."

"You're Kevin, right?" Before he could nod, she said, "And what, I should be with you now?"

Kevin was still feeling the effects of the Ecstasy. He smiled at her. "You should be with who you choose to be with. But right now, you look like you just need to have some fun. That's my specialty."

For a brief moment, a look of amazement crossed Jessica's face, as if she was impressed by his boldness. This was quickly replaced by a dark indifference. "Whatever. Sure, let's have some fun."

Kevin held up a finger. "Wait here. And if Lee finds you, just ignore him." He raced off in an awkward crowd-dodging run. He had to find Randy and Quinn.

As he ran away, Elizabeth grabbed Jessica's arm. "He's such a stoner. What are you doing?"

Kevin returned to the front door in two minutes, forcibly grabbed Jessica's hand and dragged her away from her friend.

They ended up on a back deck, looking at a communal garden shared by the entire block of Victorians. Kevin spotted a lounge chair—someone liked to sunbathe. He dropped into the chair and beckoned her to join him. She eagerly lowered herself, draped across him. For a moment, Kevin thought she was going to launch into a tirade of how horrible her boyfriend was. He was prepared to listen and endure and intersperse her complaints with notions of agreement.

Instead, she immediately leaned in and kissed him. He was surprised for a moment, but then closed his eyes and went for it. In moments, she was forcing her tongue into his mouth. His lips were tingling from the ecstasy, and his tongue trembled at the moist touch of hers. He managed to snake his arms around her, and he released his hands to freely roam her skinny body.

After a couple minutes of this, he pulled back gently from kiss. He had been getting into it, and his retreat left her with tongue hanging out of her mouth like a panting dog. He used this opportunity to place on her tongue the second pill he'd procured from Quinn.

She froze a second, and her eyes fluttered open. In the dark, he thought he saw them go cross-eyed to check her tongue, see what he was giving her. But then she pulled her tongue in to consume the pill. She leaned back in and locked her lips to his again.

Time for some real fun, he thought. He resumed pawing her body, hands creeping to every vital part that he wanted to investigate.

This went on for several minutes—until she was suddenly yanked away from him. Kevin looked up to see Lee towering over him. He grabbed her arm and pulled her to her feet. "Jess, what the hell are you doing? This guy's a freaking stoner!"

Jessica stumbled a moment before catching her balance. She suddenly laughed at her boyfriend. "See, Lee, I can be a skank too."

"Shut up!"

Kevin managed to jump to his feet. "What's the big deal, Piker? You don't want her anyway."

"You've already earned an ass-kicking, Donner!" Lee yelled. "You trespassed on another man's property."

Jess threw her arm out, wrenching it from Lee's grip. "I am not your property!"

"And you're not much of a man," Kevin grinned. "Big jock—"

Piker suddenly swung, his powerful fist impacting the side of Kevin's skull. Kevin reeled, landed on his knees on the lawn chair. The punch sent more colors reeling through his brain, different colors from what ecstasy showed him. Strange, he thought, isn't a punch to the face supposed to hurt? He found some kind of resolve deep down and managed to rise steadily to his feet. He spotted a small flowerpot sitting on a ledge next to a window. He grabbed it and swung.

The pot smashed over Lee's skull, showering both Lee and Jessica with damp potting soil. Lee stumbled back. Kevin stepped in like a focused robot. He swung a fist in what he believed was an uppercut. It shattered Piker's nose. The jock flew backward, landed on his back, holding his broken face. Blood poured between his fingers.

Kevin the robot moved in deliberately. He knelt down and began swinging, punch after punch landing against Piker's face. He tried to knock aside the hands that were holding the broken nose, and Piker found himself trying to dodge and block those punches. One fist clipped his eye, and he saw stars.

Kevin kept swinging. Somewhere in the back of his mind, he registered the reactions of the crowd, cheering the fight. He also saw the cuts opening on Piker's face, becoming bloodier and bloodier.

"Get off him!" he heard Jessica screaming. Then he felt someone, multiple someones, grabbing his arms and dragging him away. When he was pulled away, Jessica swooped in, kneeling over her cad of a beau.

Kevin took a breath, sagged in his captors' arms.

Jessica stood and confronted him, tears in her eyes. "What's wrong with you? He's all messed up! What's wrong with you?"

"What's the big deal?" Kevin said. "He's a dick."

With Kevin still held back, she suddenly slapped him across the face. The crowd emitted a sudden collective jeer. She then turned and dropped to her knees, cradling Piker's head. Kevin's last sight was her crying and whispering desperately for him to be OK.

As Kevin was dragged back toward the house, he suddenly got a look at the scene he had caused. The back deck was loaded with partygoers, and several had brought out their cell phones to get video of the attack. "Let's get you out of here," one of his captors said. It was Randy. He and Quinn pulled him back inside. Kevin registered more onlookers, partygoers watching as he was dragged through the crowds and out the front door.

"Dude, just split," Quinn urged them. "Go home. In case they call the cops or something. I'm out of here."

Quinn took off up the street. Randy led Kevin in the other direction.

When they had put some distance behind them, Randy suddenly burst out, "Dude, did you see him? He was all kinds of tore up. They're going to be talking about you."

Kevin shrugged. "What the hell? He was such a jerk to her. What's the big deal?"

* * *

"How many movies have you seen where potheads are depicted as just the amiable, dumb, harmless dudes that just sit around and laugh about stupid shit?" Steve asked Suzy. "We've been socially engineered as a society to believe that those lovable losers are the norm. I've seen something far different. I've come across some suspects that are downright belligerent and hostile. Since Prop 64 passed, every time I encounter a pothead in the course of the job... things are different. They've been bombarded with the legalization campaign. They go to these fake doctors that advertise that they can "get legal." The department has taken a step back from marijuana enforcement. No one is telling them that there are still rules. So when I try to clarify those rules, they want to get in my face, they want to take me on. They don't care about the badge. Because now we're supposedly taking away their "right." And all I want is for them to follow the rules." Steve took a breath. "I don't see the lovable losers. I see the psychosis taking hold of them. Therein lies the real danger."

Sitting across from him on the couch, Suzy said, "I have to admit, I've come across that a few times myself. And because I'm a woman, they think they can take me down easier. I've had to show a few that this is not the case." She smiled. "So, what do you do every April 20th when they do Hempfest in Golden Gate Park?"

Steve rolled his eyes. "Four-twenty Day?" He paused. "When I was a rookie, I saw something that stuck with me. I worked Hemp-fest my first year. I was standing near a tent when I saw a dude burst out from the tent, screaming his head off. He stood there for a moment, his hands tearing at his face. Seconds later, his two buddies run outside and grab him, and they drag him back inside. One of them stops and looks around, like he's looking for witnesses. He saw me watching, but he hurried back inside. That told me that they were activists with something to prove, like how harmless this shit really is, and they were covering up anything that proves otherwise. They're all looking out for each other. I started to go investigate, but my FTO stopped me and just said, "Let it go." Steve rolled his eyes again but couldn't help a smile. "Ever since then, I call off that day, stay inside, lock my doors and watch action movies all day."

She leaned in and kissed him. "Enough shop talk, hero. Let's go work off some of that frustration."

CHAPTER 6

Suzy left for work earlier the next morning, leaving Steve to sleep a short while longer. When he was finally on his way to the 3rd Street Headquarters, Steve received word of another cannabis dispensary burglary. The address was a few blocks north of Golden Gate Park, on Geary Street. Steve sent out a mass text to his teammates, who were likely also on their way to the station. They would meet him at the scene instead.

Steve pulled up behind a single patrol unit outside a non-descript four story building. From what he could tell, there were apartments upstairs, and the dispensary occupied a suite on the ground floor. As Steve approached, the first of his team arrived. Scot Black had circled the block and parked around the corner. He nodded to his partner as they approached. Steve glanced up at a plain sign over the door: Geary Health Concern. The 't' in Health was a small green cross. Steve pointed the sign out to his partner. "There's a contradiction in terms."

Scot shook his head and stepped inside. Steve's badge was dangling from the chain around his neck, and he pulled it out from under his shirt.

Steve recognized the two uniforms inside as having worked the burglary yesterday. They recognized him as well. The senior partner, a dark-skinned Asian officer named Pak, stepped forward. "Inspectors," he said by way of a greeting. "It's the same deal as yesterday. Someone forced the door and cleaned out everything from the counter. The place has a vault, and they tried for it, but couldn't get it open." He nodded to the skinny weathered man speaking with his partner. "That's the manager."

"Thanks, brother, we'll come talk to him in a minute." Officer Pak nodded and broke away.

Steve glanced around, seeing camera pods in two corners. "We have surveillance cameras; we can try those." As Dave and A.J. walked in, Steve said, "What are the chances that our friend Lynell pulled this job off too?"

"Considering he was released with a citation and court date," A.J. said, "I'd say it's a strong possibility."

"I have his address," Steve said, "we can pick him up for questioning."

"Not to be the wet blanket," Scot brought up, "but we should probably do our investigation before we assign the crime to a suspect."

Steve smiled and turned toward where the uniforms were entertaining the shop owner.

He stopped short when he saw the expression on Officer Pak's face. Pak had raised a hand to the earpiece connected to his radio. "Inspectors, we're getting word, 211 silent alarm. On Post, just east of 101. Witness just called 911, it looks like a takeover robbery. It's another dispensary."

"Oh, shit," Steve said, "I know that place. My guys, let's go!"

Special Forces filed out to their vehicles. Steve observed two uniforms from one of the patrol units running to their car as well. Steve had a red and blue light device in his SUV, but he knew the others did not have such a device in their personal vehicles. "I'm rolling code," he announced to his men. "Scot, ride with me. The rest of you, just get there quick. Maybe we can catch a suspect."

Steve jumped into his SUV and got them underway. The black-and-white pulled out, a burst of siren piercing the neighborhood. With Steve driving, Scot pulled the light device from the center console and placed it on the dash. Steve had a siren installed in the SUV and Scot activated that too. The black-and-white took a quick right turn onto Geary Street, and Steve spun his steering wheel to turn with them. With the patrol unit breaking trail, they sped eastward toward the robbery scene.

"Text the guys," Steve said. "It's called "The Greenery," one block east of 101 on Post Street. Straight shot down Geary."

Scot tapped the screen of his phone. He scoffed. "The Greenery?"

Steve scoffed right back. "Yeah, I love how these places all have such healthy innocent names. I know the place, I discovered it during my research for this operation. It's a four-story apartment building with some businesses on the ground floor. A couple of those businesses have shut down or moved because of all the nuisance problems from the pot shop."

As Steve sped them down Geary Street, Scot turned on the police radio mounted low between the dash and center console. They listened as messages from units approaching the crime scene began to come in. "David-twelve, still four minutes out. We'll start the perimeter." They could hear his siren in the background of the broadcast.

"David-Forty-one," Steve recognized Officer Pak's voice, "We're also about four minutes out. Twelve, suggest you reduce to Code 2. We may have suspects inside, don't want to give ourselves away yet."

"Ten-four." The siren in the background was now gone.

"Good idea," Scot said and turned off Blazer's siren.

Steve followed the patrol unit as they weaved in and out of traffic. The midmorning roadways were occupied but not terribly crowded at this time. The black-and-white ahead of them navigated the streets easily and for the most part, the vehicles on the street parted for them. Pak slowed his patrol vehicle at every intersection, then rushed through, with Blazer's black SUV on his heels. Several times, cars were reluctant to move from the intersection, prompting officers to chirp their siren without putting it on full blast. Each time, Steve was fortunate enough to be able to swiftly follow before motorists could clog the roads again. With Steve driving an unmarked vehicle, even with the lights and sirens he'd installed, there was a danger of a motorist not recognizing his as a police vehicle. Thinking that the passing emergency vehicle was alone, any motorist could decide that the danger was over and pull out in front of him; in fact, it happened twice during this trip. Each time, Steve had to react quickly with an evasive turn and skirt the unsuspecting vehicle.

They soon crossed Highway 101 and Pak radioed that they had arrived. Steve jumped into the conversation. "David-Twelve, Forty-one, this is Wild Boy One. You guys close off each end of the block. We will go in on foot and assess." Ahead of them, Officer Pak pulled his vehicle to the side of the road and inched his way out into the intersection. David-Twelve had already arrived, and he radioed that he had closed off the east end of the block. Pak rolled his car into the intersection and stopped, blocking the roadway. One last car remained on the block, driving through, and Pak got out to frantically motion them past his vehicle. Other units were on the way, and they would be directed to other perimeter positions.

Steve stopped his vehicle short of the intersection. Scot had already prepared their tactical vests, which were sitting on the back seat. They jumped from the SUV and quickly donned those vests. There wasn't much in the way of extra equipment on these vests, just a few spare magazines for their SIG Sauer side-arms. It took them only seconds to get ready.

Steve led his partner to the corner of the building. He peeked around, saw no obvious danger. He nodded to Scot, and they broke from cover headed to where Steve knew the front door would be.

This block had a couple of non-descript buildings, simple tan concrete structures. The building with the Greenery took up much of the block. Steve eyed the streets around them, searching for any threats, anything that might be related to the suspects thought to still be inside. He then checked the sidewalk in front of him. There was no cover between them and front door to the shop. One possible positive he saw, the suite next door to the Greenery was vacant, which might offer them a bit of safety in their approach, if necessary—.

The door to the Greenery suddenly burst open. A young woman burst out, black with colored braids weaved into her hair. "Help!" she screamed, "Somebody help me!"

Steve stopped suddenly, bringing up his gun, but in an instant, he took his finger off the trigger. She was facing the other way, hadn't seen them yet. "Police," he announced himself.

She spun around and froze when she saw them.

"Stop right there," Steve calmly told her.

"Help me!" she said, "We were just attacked and

robbed. My boss is inside. They beat him down and tied him up.

"Ma'am," Steve said calmly but firmly, "We will check inside. I need you to follow my instructions, for your safety and mine. I need you to turn and face away from me." She was shaking with fear and frustration, Steve could see, but she did comply. "Good. I need you to put your hands behind your head...Walk backwards toward me."

She was just yards away and closed the distance quickly. Steve holstered his weapon, and Scot stepped aside, his gun at low ready to cover the woman, who was obviously not a threat. But they couldn't take any chances yet. While covering her, Scot also kept an eye on the front door to the Greenery, ready if another suspicious person came out. Holding his gun with one hand, Scot motioned toward Pak's unit.

Steve gave the woman a cursory search, careful not to do anything sexually untoward. He distracted her with questions. "How many people still inside?"

"Just him. The robbers left a few minutes ago."

"Where did they leave him?"

"There's a door behind the counter, leads to a back room. He's in there. Please help him."

"We will." Steve elected not to cuff the woman. He looked at Black.

Scot had holstered and met Pak. "Looks like suspects are GOA," he said. "Put her in your car, we'll talk with her once we've cleared the building. Start an ambulance."

With that, Steve handed the woman off to Pak, who quickly shuffled her away. Both Special Forces cops once again drew their weapons as they ran to the front door of the Greenery.

Steve edged in closer to the building, aiming for the front door. He examined it quickly from the side and saw that it opened inward. Not the best way to make entry, but their options and time were limited. They'd been told the bad guys had already fled, but...

Steve stepped into the open and pushed his body against the glass door. He was stepping through a window to hell, where he was an easy target for anyone inside waiting to kill. No one shot at him. He entered and played his gun over the interior of the shop. He drifted right, and Scot moved left.

The shop was just like any other, with the walls painted black and white, and glass counters set at a right angle pointing away from the door. They found the lobby clear of any threats. Steve quickly approached the counter and leaned over with his gun, checking for anyone lurking there, but found the area empty.

"Doorway," Scot said, nodding behind the counter.

Steve nodded. He edged behind the counter through a swinging gate. From a place of cover next to the door, Steve pushed it gently, found that it swung easily, and gave it a shove. The door thumped against the wall. Steve scoped the inside, top to bottom. It was dark, but the darkness was still. At the bottom, he confirmed a body, right where the woman said he would be.

"One down," Steve said. "Check him." He stepped over the body and continued down the hall. There were two more doors visible in the darkness, both standing open. The first was lit, and he recognized some kind of vault, with a large cage and a heavy outer door. The cage was also open. He moved on briefly to the second room. It was a break room and it reeked of marijuana smoke. Then again, the whole shop did. He returned to the vault room to give it a more thorough examination.

"Blazer, this guy's alive," Scot called out.

Steve backed away from the vault. He met Scot's glance. "We're clear. I'll get paramedics in here." In passing, he got a better look at the victim. He was a black male, rolled slightly to one side because his hands were tied behind his back.

Steve hurried to the door but took the time to pause there and gently push it open without exiting. "All clear," he shouted. He then stepped outside, and again shouted, "All clear!"

The moment he appeared, movement to his left grabbed his attention. Dave and A.J. stepped out from behind one of two patrol units at the corner and ran toward him. One of those black-and-whites briefly screeched tires to speed from the intersection and park in front of the shop. When Pak stepped out, Steve shouted to him, "We need an ambulance, one down inside, still breathing."

Pak nodded and shouted back, "It's on the way."

Steve pulled his men aside. "A.J., go inside and cover Black. Get a look at the crime scene, see if there's anything we might be able to use to find a suspect." A.J. nodded and jogged toward the door. Steve turned to Dave. "We've got a witness out here, let's go talk to her."

* * *

A.J. poked his head into the shop. "Yo, Scotty!"

"Back here," Scot answered.

A.J. scoped out the shop as he crossed to the swinging gate. He saw Scot crouched in the open doorway over the victim. "Ambulance is on the way," he said, "How is he?"

"He's got some head trauma," Scot answered. "He was tied up with some thin rope. I cut it off to preserve the knot. Didn't want to move him too much in case of spine injury."

A.J. nodded. In the darkness, he saw that Scot had slipped on a pair of latex gloves. A.J. carried some with him in a coat pocket for just such an occasion, and he quickly pulled them on. Scot had placed the cut rope against the wall next to him. A.J. leaned down to pick the strands up, but Scot said, "Leave them for now, let CSI bag it from there."

"Got it." A. J. retreated to the lobby to get a better look at the damage. Like the last place, there were glass display cases, all of which were shattered. It appeared that many of the shop's samples were displayed in clear plastic envelopes. Many of those empty envelopes were scattered among the broken glass. A.J. ran a cursory eye over all of it. "I suppose it's too much to ask to find a discarded crowbar," he joked.

* * *

Outside, Steve sought out the woman who had flagged them down. She'd been placed in the back of a patrol car at the west end of the block. As Steve approached, he saw that the two officers from that unit were standing outside the car. The woman inside was yelling, at them and at every cop in a ten block radius.

Steve eyed the uniforms as he approached. "Sorry, Sarge," one of them said. "We had to step out for a moment. She was starting to get racial about us evil cops treating black people like criminals."

Steve rolled his eyes and sighed. "Let me see if I can calm her down." He stepped up to the patrol car and opened the back door. Ugly words spilled out.

"And here's the head pig. Want to treat a woman like a suspect 'cause she's a niggah. Meanwhile, another niggah's dying in there. I will have your badge for this, bitch!"

Steve crouched next to the door, dropping down next to her so she actually looked down at him from her seat inside the car. "Can we talk now? I need your help."

"Oh, now you me to help you?"

A siren chirping clipped the conversation for a moment. An ambulance had arrived on scene and maneuvered past their patrol car to enter the block. Steve nodded to the van as it stopped in front of the Greenery. "They're here for your boss. He's alive, and he might just make it. I'm sorry we met under such crazy circumstances. You have to understand, as cops, we're coming into this situation blind. We don't know who's coming out of that store, we don't know who's inside, and we don't know who the real bad guys are yet. We don't know who the threat is, so we have to treat everyone as a threat. We can work out who's who later on when everything is under more control. But it really is for your safety, as well as ours, that we approached you like that. I think things have calmed down now. I really do need your help."

The woman had finally shut up and was now in tears. The stress was finally catching up to her.

Steve stood, seeing that she was not handcuffed. "I'll tell you what. Why don't we get you out of the back of the police car?" He stood back and offered her a hand. The crying had progressed, and she was now shaking. She hesitated, then finally reached out and took his hand. Steve pulled gently, letting her rise to her full five-foot five height.

Steve faced another quick choice, whether to question her within sight of the shop, and risk her suddenly running to her boss's side when he was wheeled out or interview her around the corner to keep her from getting distracted. Still holding her hand, led toward the wall of the three-story building adjacent the Greenery, where they were out of sight.

"First, can I get your name?"

"Shayquanda. Shayquanda Neill."

"Thank you, Miss Neill." He'd keep it professional, not trying to mangle pronunciation of her first name. "What's your boss's name?"

"Walter Coggins."

"Thank you. Can you walk me through what happened?"

"I just got back from lunch. I was putting some more samples under the counter. These two niggahs walked in. They had these hoodies on."

"You made a reference just now," Steve interrupted her. "I don't want to use that ugly word, but did you mean you could tell their race?"

"Yeah!" She didn't seem to care about her own use of the word. "I could tell by the voice. They was brothas."

"OK. Can you give me any description of them?"

"I couldn't see they faces," she said. "They had the hoods up and pulled closed. But I know they was brothas. They had black jeans. Loose fitting, like they was supposed to sag. But they wasn't sagging."

"What color were the hoodies?"

"Like a dark gray."

"You said you heard their voices. What did they say?"

"One of them stuck a big black gun in my face. He said 'don't move, bitch'. Then he said to his partner, "Do it." His partner started smashing the glass counters. My boss came at him and tried to stop them, but they smacked him upside the head, and... and they just started beating him."

Dave stepped into the conversation. "Is there anything else you can give us regarding a description? Was he short? Tall?"

"He was tall. Over six feet. And he was really

thick, like he was all muscle."

"What about the second suspect?"

"I don't know." She started to tear up again.

"OK," Steve said. "Miss Neill, you really have been very helpful." He gestured to Officer Pak. "This officer is going to get some more information from you and then you're free to go. We'll contact you about an official statement. I'm sure you probably want to accompany Walter to the hospital, and I'm sure he'd appreciate it."

He handed her off to Pak and stepped away. Scot and A.J. were just exiting the shop, right behind the paramedics, who were now loading their gurney with Walter Coggins. The four of them gathered near the shop's entrance.

Steve glanced at A.J., who said, "There's nothing obvious like last time. We'll have to hope CSI finds something we can go on."

"I still like Lynell for this one and probably the 459 at the first one," Steve said. "To me, it looks like he was unable to get into vaults during the burglaries, so he steps up to robbery for direct access. He's getting ballsier. Let's find him and bring him in for a voice lineup with Miss Neill. Maybe we'll get lucky."

"So now, fearless leader," Scot brought up, "Where do we find him?"

* * *

Kevin entered the alley, dreading the next part of his day. His day had been full of dread. He'd gotten up early this morning, a rare feat for him, and even rarer since he'd been out late after the party last night. But he wanted to avoid contact with his parents, or he'd have to endure more lectures about his run-in with the cops. He left for school early. More dread awaited him there, as he wondered what the fall out would be for him beating down a jock. As he walked up the steps to the main entrance, he detected the looks from the students he passed. They all seemed to look at him, gauging him, as if wondering what kind of person he really was, if he could take on someone like that jock, Lee.

The looks had become more prevalent as he walked the hallways. People would stop in the hall and watch him walk by, turn from their lockers to track his passage. He stared at one guy as walked by, then suddenly turned around and found someone else looking. The looks seemed to come from everywhere. He passed one group at their lockers, who actually turned from their conversation and stared at him. "What?" he said to them, then shouted, "What?" Several others in the hallway stopped to look at his outburst.

Randy Shepherd's voice called from down the hallway, "Dude!"

Randy shoved his way through the hallway, grabbed Kevin and dragged him into a nearby boy's room. He quickly looked through the bathroom, shoving stalls open to make sure none were occupied. "I am amazed you showed your face here today."

"How bad is it?"

"Lee didn't show up for school today. Rumor is he's in the hospital. The football team...They want to kick your ass. No, they want to freaking kill you."

Kevin breathed a curse.

"They've already hit me up in the hall upstairs, wanting to know where you are," Randy went on. "I didn't tell them anything. But listen, you can't stay here. They'll find you. You might as well ditch today."

Kevin breathed deep again. "Yeah, I think you're right."

"Awesome. I'll go with you. Wait here." Shepherd poked his head out into the hallway. "We're clear," he whispered, "let's go."

It had been surprisingly easy for them to make their escape. They were not stopped by any teacher or administrator. They walked the streets until they reached Randy's house in Coe Valley. Frequently during their walk, Shepherd promised an afternoon of getting stoned and playing video games, since his parents were still not home.

When they had walked into the house, Randy had said, "Wait in the living room. I have something for you."

Returning home now as the sun was setting, Kevin slipped into the back yard and quietly slid open the sliding door. Immediately, his parents' voices assaulted him from the next room. He padded noiselessly down the hallway without them seeing him. He quietly closed his bedroom door.

He took out the half-used package of cigarillos. He'd smoked two blunts at Randy's and had one more cigarillo left. He set the package on his already cluttered nightstand and reached into his backpack for the prize that Randy had given him.

His bedroom door suddenly burst open. He dropped the backpack as his Dad suddenly towered in the doorway. "Yeah, he's here," he called out to his wife. "We have to talk, kid."

"This is my room," Kevin screamed, "You can't just barge in here!"

"I own this house, kid. I make the rules. And since you were busted by the cops last night—and then snuck out after I grounded you—we have to discuss your actions. Actions have consequences, Kevin."

"Consequences? I told you the thing with the cops was no big deal."

"Anything with the cops is a big deal. Don't you get that?" His dad's eyes fell to the cigarillo packet. "This shit has got to stop too. This is why you're failing in school."

"Come on, dad, I told you, that teacher has it in for me. It's not my fault."

"It's never your fault," his dad shook his head. "Kevin, every choice you make has a consequence." He picked up the cigarillo pack. "This is a bad choice. Smoking weed is going to damage you."

"Please," Kevin scoffed, "This shit's practically legal."

"It's still a drug, Kevin."

"What's the big deal? You smoke it!"

Kevin saw the sudden look on his Dad's face and could only describe it as cold shock. His voice lowered to the most chilling growl he'd ever heard. "Do you have any idea how much damage it has done to me? Do you have any idea how much I regret taking that first drag? Now I'm addicted, and I can't quit!"

Kevin lay back on his bed, a dark look frozen on his face. His entire shitty life was falling in on him. And his parents didn't even know about the fight yet.

His dad tossed the cigarillos back onto the nightstand. "Tomorrow we're going to your school. I'll be meeting with your principal, and any teacher that's available. We're going to figure out what work you've missed, and you're going to start trying to catch up."

The ice on Kevin's face broke as his eyes shot wide open. Not only was he being forced to go to school, where the football team wanted to kill him, but his dad would be there, and would find out more about his son than he ever wanted to know.

"You're not to leave this room until dinner. If you have homework with you, now is a good time to do it." He backed out the door and quietly closed it.

"Shit," Kevin whispered, sitting up. He glanced around his room. Was he just coming down from his earlier blunt, or were these walls actually closing in on him?

He grabbed his backpack and reached inside. Grabbing Randy's gift made him feel momentarily powerful, but the feeling was just momentary. He pulled it out, holding it with two hands.

Randy had lent him his dad's silver revolver.

He was ready for the football team now.

He could deal with them now. It was being here that he couldn't deal with. He suddenly stuffed the gun back into his backpack. He grabbed the bag, and in seconds had escaped out his window.

* * *

"How did you find him before?" Scot asked.

Steve's answer was, "I got lucky."

The team had gathered outside the apartment building that was listed as Lynell's address of record. Rather than go barging upstairs to drag their suspect in for questioning on thin evidence and even thinner probable cause, they conferred outside on a possible strategy. Steve knocked, Scot at his side, and Dave and A.J. covering any back exits to an alley behind the building. When there was no answer, Steve elected not to kick in the door yet. Downstairs, they conferenced again.

"When I found his print and got the name, I came here. I wanted as much intel as I could before I went up there," Steve explained. "You see the vehicles on the street here, well, I picked a few that might be fancy enough for a drug dealer. You recall the shiny Chrysler 300 he was driving? It was parked right over there," he pointed. "Seemed like the obvious choice. Before I could go knock, he came outside, so I just followed him."

"Considering that," Scot said, "We still don't have enough to arrest, let alone detain."

"And he'll just lawyer up when we do bring him

in," Steve agreed. "But I still want to bring him in. More and more, I think he's doing these burglaries, and now he's graduated to robbery." Steve thought for a moment. "There is one possibility. When he was released last night, I was there to meet him. He was picked up by a black female driving a tan Toyota. I memorized her plate. Maybe we can run it, track her down and ask her assistance."

He pulled out his smart phone and opened an app that connected him to SFPD's databases. He was able to put in the license plate, and in moments had an address. "Loqueesha Betts," he shared with the team and said, "Let's go."

They travelled six blocks to an apartment building just off of Geary, near San Francisco City College. By now, it was late in the afternoon and the sun was going down making long shadows from the buildings all around them. They parked on the street. As Steve stepped out, he was already eyeing their surroundings. He nodded at Scot, toward a vehicle parked nearby. "There's the Toyota. But I don't see his Chrysler 300 here."

Dave and A.J. joined them. "There's a fire escape on both sides of the building."

"OK, I'll have you guys cover one each and Scot and I will go knock. We don't have our radios, so I'll conference call everyone."

They dispersed to their assignments. Steve and Scot approached the building, mounted the steps. They found a security gate mounted over the front door and a key panel that demanded an access code. Steve was about to start pressing all buttons, but then on a whim tugged on the door. It wasn't latched. "So much for security," he whispered. They entered.

Trying to be quiet, they climbed the steps to the third floor of four. Steve quietly checked door numbers in the dim hallway. It appeared there were only two units per floor and the one belonging to Lynell's girlfriend was on the north side. Scot pulled out his phone and quickly dialed the numbers of both partners outside. "North side," Scot said to everyone on the conference call.

"That's me," Dave answered, "I've got it."

Scot nodded to Blazer. Steve turned and knocked firmly on the door.

They heard a faint thumping noise inside, then nothing for a moment. Steve pounded again.

An angry voice inside shouted, "Who is it?"

"Police, Loqueesha," Steve announced.

There was another pause, and she suddenly opened the door a crack, letting the security chain stop it. "What the hell do you want?"

Steve flashed his badge. "Sergeant Blazer, SFPD. We're looking for Lynell Richards."

"He ain't here." She pinned him with a devastating look that seemed to say, 'what else you got?'

"Loqueesha Betts?" His knowing her name seemed to disarm her a little bit, and Steve asked, "You were seen picking him up from County Jail yesterday. Where did you take him?"

Before she could answer, Scot suddenly said, "Bedroom window."

Steve decided quickly that a fleeing suspect was enough exigent circumstances to force entry. "Step back," he demanded of Betts. He shouldered the door, ripping the chain from the frame.

Betts stepped back, almost stumbled over the mess on her floor. "Get out of my house!" she screamed.

Steve raced across her living room, which had food wrappers and other trash strewn over the floor and any flat furniture surface. He spotted a doorway to his left and maneuvered toward it. He paused in the doorway, seeing the open window. Richards was already outside.

He turned back to the front door.

"He's going up!" Scot relayed Dave's message.

"Stairs!" Steve responded, headed out the door.

They retreated to the stairway they had just come up and started toward the fourth floor. Steve continued up, where the stairs ascended into a small enclosure with walls painted a drab gray. The door to the outside was on a small landing. Steve bounded up to it and flattened the push bar. He ran his whole body into the door when it refused to open for him. He cursed in a moment of frustration and anger. He stepped back, grabbed the railing and kicked at the door. It was a normal door, not sturdy as it should have been, but it did not give. He kicked again.

* * *

Outside, Dave was straining to see through the growing darkness. He knew the apartment was on the third floor, so he scanned those windows. A couple of them had lights on, and he watched for any movement...

A human form suddenly rolled out one window, briefly blocking the light and giving himself away. "He's coming out the bedroom window on my side," Dave said over his phone. He stepped toward the spot where the second floor fire escape ladder was mounted. When Richards reached it, it would pivot down, and Dave would be waiting. "Police! Come on down, Richards!"

The running form stopped at the stairs leading down. In the darkness, Dave couldn't see his face. Richards suddenly reversed.

"He's going up," Dave said into his phone. "I'm going after him."

Dave ran to the spot where the ladder waited. He jumped up and grabbed onto what would be the bottom rung. He let his body weight pivot the ladder down, and then mounted the steps. When he reached the second floor, the ladder automatically folded on its spring mechanism back into position. Dave glanced up, seeing Lynell near the top. He left his gun in its holster for now and climbed those steps as fast as he could.

He reached the top in seconds. Standing on the ladder, he kept his body tucked below the safety wall. He yanked out the gun and rose quickly, playing the gun over the roof as he searched for the suspect.

There was no immediate sign of Lynell. Dave used one hand to pull himself up, the other holding the gun. Once onto the roof, he stepped out into the open, searching.

A thumping noise drew him, and he skirted a large air vent. Someone had set up a kind of garden on the roof, with numerous potted plants grouped together. On the other side, he found the structure that was the stairway entry. The thumping was someone pounding on the door from inside. It was probably Blazer, he realized.

The swish of a plant moving reached him and he turned toward the garden. Richards suddenly loomed in front of him. Dave was unprepared, and Richards landed a punch to his jaw. Dave stumbled back but managed to keep his feet. Richards moved in again, swung, and landed another punch to his eye.

This time, Dave went down. His gun skidded across the gravel surface of the roof. He was dazed, but he yanked his faculties back, and crawled quickly to where the gun landed. He did not want Richards to get control of the gun, lest he shoot the cop with his own weapon.

Dave grabbed the gun, and swung into a crouch, aiming at where his attacker had come from. But Richards had fled instead, and Dave saw the suspect jump over the retaining wall.

Still dazed, Dave surged weakly to his feet, headed for that wall. He heard a smashing noise, and Blazer and Black suddenly burst from the stairwell onto the roof. Steve saw Dave stumbling to the wall and took in the bleeding cut over his left eye.

"Castillo! You OK?"

Dave stumbled to the wall and looked over. The next building was tucked up next to this one, the roof just one floor below. "He went that way."

"What happened?" Scot asked, taking in his partner's appearance.

Dave turned from the wall, and leaned back against it, taking a moment to catch his breath. "He came out of nowhere," he waved weakly at the garden with his gun, then holstered it. "He only hit me twice. That son of a bitch is strong."

Steve glanced over the neighboring roof, but now needed to make the wellbeing of his man a priority. He saw a bench sitting next to the garden and pulled Dave toward it. "Here, sit down. I want you checked out by medics."

"Boss, I'm fine. You're the one in the middle, right?"

"Right." He gestured at Black. Scot had already requested Miano to "get your ass up here," now that their suspect was in the wind.

A.J. arrived in one minute. Steve directed him to assist Dave downstairs to await the ambulance. They could already hear the siren approaching. To Scot, he said, "Let's you and I pay a visit to Loqueesha. I want to bring her in for questioning."

* * *

Three hours later, Steve and Scot had released Loqueesha. She'd volunteered no information even after they tried putting the fear of God into her.

Even as they kicked her loose, Steve couldn't resist escorting her out to the Mission Rock Station lobby. She tried to ignore him as she broke away and headed out the lobby door. As she slipped out the door, Steve received a text. Dave and A.J. were returning from the hospital. Steve wanted to watch or even follow Loqueesha, see if anyone picked her up, like maybe Lynell. But would he be that dumb?

As he checked the text, the nearby elevator chimed. A casual glance that way turned him into a guided missile when he saw who stepped out. "Lawyer Kline!"

The short Assistant District Attorney had made a beeline for the front desk, hidden behind its recently installed plexi-glass. He froze, hearing his name and recognizing who approached. "Sergeant."

"I just want to update you on my progress," Steve began. "You remember that burglary suspect you released for committing a 'misdemeanor' break-in? He's now graduated to armed 211 and attempted murder. He held up a marijuana dispensary and put the manager in the hospital. I believe those are still felonies, are they not?"

"I didn't write the law, Sergeant."

"Maybe. But can we admit that this law was a lie to begin with? And that it is having the opposite effect of what it was supposed to?"

"Is this more about your demon weed?" Steve wondered if the sneer on his face came naturally, or if he did it solely for sarcasm purposes.

"I'm sure you know that Prop 47 was sold to the public as a way to reduce the sentences of 'Non-violent' drug offenders. That's a whole other category, but what they didn't tell us was that it actually reduced the sentences of most crimes. Many crimes that used to be felonies are now misdemeanors—and yes, many of those crimes are violent. What I see, counselor, is people committing crimes and having no consequence, which means they keep committing bigger and bigger crimes until they finally do something bad enough for the state to say enough is enough." He stared down the lawyer's incredulous look. "That's where my suspect is now. Because he was let go on the non-violent burglary, he was free to commit an armed robbery and now put a cop, my officer, in the hospital."

"Sergeant, I'm sorry your man was injured. Bring me a suspect and an airtight case, and we'll put your suspect away."

"Count on it."

Steve pinned him with a mean glare. But since there was no further tirade, Kline took the opportunity to slink away.

Steve looked away from the retreating lawyer as someone else approached. Captain Stanson walked up with another man, and Steve could see right away he was a man of the streets who appeared to have moved up in the world. The man had the weathered face of someone in his forties but carried himself like a much younger man. He wore pressed khakis and a polo shirt, and Steve noted the automatic on his hip. He also carried an ID badge issued by SFPD, so he must be OK.

Stanson stared after Kline, who had reached the door and fled the conversation, but he did not mention the ADA. "Sergeant Steve Blazer, meet Agent Shaver of the DEA."

Hearing where the stranger came from, Steve immediately tried to size up the situation. Why was Stanson putting him with a DEA Agent? He stayed silent for a moment, waiting to see where this spur of the moment meeting was going.

Shaver stuck out his hand, and Blazer curiously shook it. "I hear you're doing some interesting work here in town."

Steve narrowed his brow, betraying his suspicion. "And this has drawn the interest of the DEA?"

"It's drawn *my* interest. If you've got a moment, I'd like to brief you on a few things."

Steve gave a slight shrug. "OK."

Shaver started his briefing right there in the lobby. "DEA has really taken a back seat with the legalization. The public thinks it's harmless, and more and more states are starting to legalize or decriminalize, so DEA has not tried to crack down federally. I think someone in Washington is waiting for the administration to put out some directives as to which way they lean on the issue."

"They toyed with federally legalizing under Obama," Steve said, "and everyone wanted DEA to reschedule and reclassify pot. I don't see it happening under this President."

Shaver nodded. "I've been watching the legalization campaign roll right along. I've watched what happened with Colorado and Washington and the subsequent problems that no one wants to talk about. I'm seeing some of those same problems arise with California's legalization. They decriminalized under Governor Schwarzenegger, so people have been able to have certain amounts and grow their own plants. But now, the dispensaries are opening, and everyone's hoping to make big bucks, including the state of California. But, if people are growing their own, how much business will the dispensaries actually do?"

"So, your interest here is purely financial?" Steve asked.

"No. Jeez, are you always this cynical?"

"I come by it honestly."

"Well, then what I have to say may add to your cynicism. One part of the law was supposed to limit pot farms to one acre. They released new regs last month and that language is gone. That opened the door for several large companies to swoop in and set up mass farms of large acreage. This is going to have several consequences. It may dilute the market, it may lead to inferior product. And it freezes out the small businesses trying to make a go of this. Several dispensaries around town have already been bought out by big companies looking to corner the market. From my research, Green Resolve is not one of them.

Steve noted the other members of his team entering the lobby. Scot had met Dave and A.J. outside as they returned from the hospital. Steve saw them and nodded them over. They approached the gathering, quietly joining. Steve did not yet introduce his men. "My goal this week has been twofold: first, to remove as much product from the street because I know how harmful it is; second, I want to try and show some of the offenders that, while weed may be legal, there are still rules to follow. Once the legalization takes effect January 2nd, this city can get as high as they want, as long as they follow the rules. But until then, I'm going to do everything I can to minimize the damage this city is about to do to itself."

"Sergeant, I'm trying to tell you. I agree with you. This legalization is going to have a major detrimental effect on this state. I've personally had Green Resolve under surveillance for a couple weeks now. In fact, I watched you take down the guy that tried to rob you the other day. Nice moves." Steve couldn't help a snicker.

"I'm sure you know that even though it's about to be legal to possess and use marijuana, there are still people that grow it illegally. There's a lot of federal forest land that rarely sees a human presence and people are growing marijuana illegally there. I believe some of that weed is finding its way into some of the dispensaries, like Green Resolve. I'm putting together an operation tomorrow that will hunt down some of those grows and destroy them. I'm inviting you to come along." He gestured at the others. "Bring your team along if you like."

Steve considered this a moment. "You've piqued my interest. But I have other problems here I need consider. We've got a felon robbing pot shops and beating people down. Something tells me that Green Resolve may be his next target." He glanced briefly at Dave. "He already put one of my guys in the hospital."

"You may be right about Green Resolve," Shaver said. "It ties in with something I'm working on, but I haven't put all the pieces together yet."

Steve huffed. "We need to find this guy, and I really think he has designs on Green Resolve. Dave, you need to stand down for a bit. Scot, why don't you and Dave pick up surveillance on the shop tomorrow. We can have black-and-whites saturate the area tonight and discourage another burglary. A.J., feel like a road trip with me tomorrow?"

Miano looked he was put on the spot. "Sure."

Steve looked at Shaver. "When and where?"

"Be at the Coast Guard Station on Yerba Buena Island tomorrow at 0600. Road trip, hell, we're going for a chopper ride."

"Where to?"

"Mendocino."

CHAPTER 7

The next morning, Steve found himself sitting inside the open side door of a Coast Guard helicopter, a Sikorsky MH-60 Jayhawk. The Jayhawk was a model based on the Navy's Seahawk, which was in turned modeled after the Army's Blackhawk helicopter. The wind in his face was cold with the altitude of less than a thousand feet and the late December climate. It was dark when he and Miano boarded the white- and red-painted Jayhawk for what he was told would be a forty-five-minute flight to their target zone. The flight took him back to his Army days, training for any type of scenario conceivable with Army Special Ops. He'd ridden many an early morning chopper into the hell zones of the Middle East during his time in the war on terror.

Now he was fighting a different war, but it was a war, nonetheless.

Steve had gone all out for this excursion. He'd dug from his storage a couple of old uniform items, digitized BDU pants and top. He carried rations and a camelback filled with water, along with a couple of extra weapons and a few hundred rounds of ammunition. Shaver had never specified his role in their operation, but he was not willing to give up his right to defend himself if something happened.

He knew from a brief conversation with A.J. that he had packed similarly, carrying extra guns and ammunition. Miano gave the aura of a city boy, someone who frequently dressed nice and wanted to look good. He was also a military reservist in an engineering unit. However, he'd elected in this case not to wear his Army uniforms. He was dressed casually, faded jeans and a plain gray T-Shirt under a plain blue windbreaker. Steve glanced at him in the vague light given off by the chopper's interior and could see he was shivering. Steve shrugged off his sympathy. He enjoyed the cold.

Since their arrival, Shaver had mostly kept to himself, limiting their conversation to directing him and A.J. where to wait. In the glow of the various panels of the cargo bay, he glanced over at Shaver. The Agent was studying a map that he'd been keeping in the cargo pocket of his BDU pants. He felt eyes upon him and glanced up at Blazer. He rose from his seat and crossed in front of a couple of his agents to sit across from Blazer. He reached up above and pulled a headset from a hook over the back of the seat. He handed it to Blazer and grabbed a second one for himself. He reached over and flicked a switch on Blazer's set, turning on the intercom and microphone.

"We're going to be concentrating on this area along the Eel River, south of Hull Mountain." He pointed at the map, and Steve noted the spot, a canyon in the Mendocino National Forest. The map was a topographical, and Steve could see the lines, indicating the mountain sides. He saw how close together those lines were in places, indicating steep terrain. "I want to do a few sweeps in the air to see if we can spot any possible grows, and then we can put down on this access road here."

"Are you sure that's a good idea?" Steve asked, "Doing an aerial sweep? From what I know about illegal grows in federal lands, someone has to work those grows, and frequently they are armed. Criss-crossing the canyon like that could alert someone that we're coming."

Shaver nodded. "I'll take that under advisement."

Steve was perturbed at the reply, but something in the comment struck him as genuine, not dismissive. He let it go for now, vowing to stay on his guard. "How did you get turned on to this location?"

The chopper's interior glow put a strange shadow over Shaver's smirk. "It's the damnedest thing. There's a campground a couple of miles down the river. People there started getting sick and visiting emergency rooms. EPA got involved and tested the water, and they found some weird pesticides, including a brand of rat poison. Someone put two and two together and notified us. I've been tracking much of the marijuana in San Francisco, kind of like you have. I volunteered to put together an op to check it out."

Steve nodded. Never having been on an operation like this, he'd read up on it before launching his crusade against black market weed and reread some of the literature he had last night. He had a good idea what they would find.

As the flight stretched on, the light outside grew brighter, and the sun finally peeked out from behind the mountains to their right rear. Now that he could see it, Steve watched the terrain below. They traveled north, crossing the San Francisco Bay and going "feet dry" over the San Pablo Bay Wildlife Refuge. They flew on over the Napa and Sonoma Valleys. In the growing daylight, he got a look at burn scars from recent wildfires. He'd read an ar-

ticle about how many of the residents in that area
whose homes were destroyed by the fires had their
own small marijuana grows indoors. He also wondered how many illegal grows had been destroyed
by the fires. Gradually, Steve saw the terrain below
fade from cities to mountains and forest, with only
occasional pockets of civilization.

The forest grew thick below, and shortly Steve
felt the chopper descending. They were soon flying
nape-of-the-earth, with the forested sides of a canyon on either side. Steve was still plugged into the
intercom, and he heard the pilot tell Shaver that they
were "Over the target zone."

Shaver acknowledged and leaned over toward the
open side door. Steve glanced at A.J. and pointed
to his eyes with two fingers, asking his partner to
watch the terrain out his side of the chopper. A.J.
nodded and turned away, scanning the forests below.

The chopper twisted and turned through the
curves of the canyon. Steve felt how tense he was,
remembering what he'd told Shaver. This low, he
expected some grower down below to start shooting
at their chopper. But he continued to scan, searching for discolor against the greenery, a debris field,
anything out of the ordinary that could indicate
something suspicious.

After traversing the canyon for several minutes,
Shaver said to the pilot, "Let's head to the access
road. We don't want to expose ourselves too much."

Steve looked at him, knowing it was already too
late for that.

In minutes, they began to orbit over a cleared
area. Steve spotted a road below, and as they got
closer saw that it was barely more than a dirt and
gravel trail. The road wound along the side of a
mountain, and to the north began to climb a steady
upgrade. In fact, this appeared to be the only really

level spot around. The chopper settled to the road.

Steve made himself the first off the bird. He pulled a silver .44 Magnum Desert Eagle pistol from a holster on his hip. Stepping away from the chopper, he trained the gun over the bushes and trees that bordered the clearing in the distance. If there was anyone tending an illegal marijuana grow nearby, they would know someone was in the area, and could either attack now and finish everyone off, or set up an ambush somewhere in the forest.

All but one of the occupants scrambled off the chopper. When A.J., Shaver and two of his DEA agents were out the door, the chopper accelerated its engines and lifted off.

"He's going to check some other areas," Shaver said of the last man on board. "I've got him on radio contact."

Steve nodded. "Where to?"

Shaver nodded across the clearing, where it appeared the land dropped off into thicker forest. "We follow the river."

He started that way, and everyone fell into line. Steve made sure he was in line behind Shaver. He had no idea what Shaver's skill levels as an observer were in this kind of wilderness environment. Blazer was plenty experienced from his years in the Army and he meant to watch over all of them in their search.

They traversed down a hillside, which was steep at times. Near the bottom, the trip turned from a simple hike to jumping from rock to rock as they approached the water, which was flowing free, filled from the recent rainstorms. Once at the water, Shaver turned the troop north. He directed his two agents to cross the river, using boulders to keep out of the swirling water. They paralleled the rest of the group walking up the river. Shaver seemed to be looking for something in particular, and Steve believed he knew what it was. For the moment, he kept his eyes on the hillside, watching for signs of civilization and any type of threat.

It took only thirty minutes for Shaver to find what he was looking for. When Steve saw him stop, he and A.J. came up to investigate. They found him staring down into a pool of standing water fed by the river flowing among the rocks.

Shaver pointed into the water, and Steve saw the hose nestled among the rocks, not even casually camouflaged. "This is going to feed our grow," he said, and pointed his finger, directing their gaze to where the hose ran up the mountainside. "They must have a pump somewhere up there." He hopped off the rocks toward shore and started up the hillside. Steve hastened to keep up with him, still watching for threats. A glance at the hose showed him that it traveled up the hill, partially covered by dirt, leaves or pine needles. It seemed to extend a great distance, and he saw that it went around a spur in the mountain.

Shaver stopped to survey the terrain, and Steve stopped next to him. "You smell that?" Blazer asked.

Shaver's nose twitched. "What is that? Skunk?"

"More like skunk weed."

The hose ran through a section of the forest with fewer trees, and in that clearing, they came across the first part of the grow. On a mostly level section of the hillside, they found rows of old tires partially buried. As they gathered to view this, Shaver said, "They'll use the tires as a planter box to get the young plants started. When they're big enough, the plants can be moved to a different area. If they don't reuse the tires, they just leave them, which creates an environmental hazard. We'll find the rest of the grow nearby. Just follow the hose." He started up the hill again.

Steve suddenly reached out and grabbed Shaver, pulled him back. "Hold on," he said. He drew the DEA Agent back toward a nearby tree.

Bewildered, Shaver allowed himself to be pulled back. "What's up?"

"Check the terrain," Steve said, glancing around. "There's a couple of good spots here that would make good ambush sites. For instance," and he pointed at the spur to their right, "the hose seems to lead right past that little hidey hole. Why don't you let me circle around and clear it for you?"

For a moment, Steve could see the wavering in Shaver's face, that he wanted to laugh off the threat. But he held back any rebuke and said, "OK."

Steve immediately broke away and raced toward the spur. He skirted the outside, climbing to where he was just below the summit. They could see what he was doing, working his way to the rear, so he could look down into the dip from behind the spur and make sure no one was hiding there.

He surveyed what he could see inside the hollow of the hill and he spotted something he immediately did not like. A single tree had fallen partially across the spur. It would provide convenient cover for a camp, or even an ambush site. Any curious law enforcement following that damn hose would walk right in front of the site, creating a convenient kill zone. As he examined the fallen tree, he saw that one could even escape after the ambush by simply climbing the hill right where he was and making a run for the nearby woods. With further scrutiny, he saw that a small branch had been pulled across the top, creating something of a shelter—it had not fallen that way on its own. Just past part of the branch, he could see muddy dirt disturbed from traffic in and out of that spot.

Could someone be there now?

Steve examined the terrain again, and in particular the trees just above the fallen one. He quietly made his way there, getting a better look at the sheltered area. He leaned against one young pine, then reached down. He grabbed a piece of the fallen branch and pulled.

The fallen branch was partially dislodged and collapsed into the hollowed hillside.

The man he'd surprised turned and spotted Steve above and behind him. He suddenly raised a silver automatic. Steve ducked back as a single shot ripped the air near his head. "Police! Drop it!" he shouted.

Automatic fire suddenly tore the tranquility of the forest.

* * *

A.J. watched as Blazer yanked the branch. The boss must be on to something, he realized, and he pulled his gun as a precaution.

When the first shot rang out, A.J. moved among the rows of tires, trying to get an angle on the fallen tree where someone had taken cover. Shaver mirrored his actions, pulling out his own sidearm.

A.J. moved into the kill zone just in time to see someone burst from the shelter of the fallen tree. He was wielding what appeared to be an AK-47. Before Miano could track on him, the subject had spotted him and rattled off a long burst.

A.J. dove to the ground as bullets kicked up mud and pine needles next to him. He glanced around him and found himself at the far end of the young-plant section. The nearest half-submerged tire provided at least some cover, and he scrambled behind it. Another burst from the AK chewed mud next to his knee. A.J. raised his pistol and squeezed off two rounds. It was fire meant to discourage the rifleman and he kept his fire aimed low, knowing Blazer was on the hillside above the shooter.

He bought himself a moment of the shooter's hesitation, just enough time to push up on the nearest tire, unearthing it from the soft dirt. He put himself behind it, giving himself at least eight inches of decent cover. He placed his gun arm just alongside the tire and was able to squeeze off another two rounds. Another burst rattled him, this time the bullets pounding the tire. A.J. knew his cover was not perfect and waited for those rounds to penetrate the tire, and then penetrate his skull.

The shooter emptied his magazine and wasted precious seconds fumbling for a fresh one. A.J. used that time to pull his tire with him as he scrambled backward. He picked out a nearby tree. When the automatic fire stopped, he rolled from the tire and rose to a knee behind the tree.

"Shaver!" he shouted. "Get to cover! Now, while he's reloading!" A burst tearing bark from his tree told him the shooter was done reloading. A.J. leaned out and rapid fired five shots. Shaver was finally able to gather himself and jump up. He fired several shots as he moved and found cover behind another tree.

A moment later, A.J. heard Shaver on the radio. "Hawkeye, this is Shaver. We've uncovered a hornet's nest here. Return to this area immediately. I need a spotter."

* * *

They had definitely heard the chopper, Steve realized, and knew someone was coming. The man shooting up at him squeezed off two more rounds. He'd ignored the fact that Steve identified himself as a cop.

The man suddenly began shouting. Steve recognized his use of Spanish, but in the noise and confusion only heard a couple of words. "Policia! ¡Ándale, ándale!"

He spotted movement forty yards up the hill, someone running into the open. While he was distracted by that movement, the suspect below fired at him once again, scarring the tree instead. Steve took a chance and leaned out for a quick shot. He aimed and hit center mass, putting the suspect into the mud.

A new sound reached his ears. Someone up the hill fired up a motorcycle engine, followed by a second. Two dirt bikes rolled into the open. One rider took off down what might have been a trail. The second made the decision to stop and shoot at the police. Steve stayed by his tree and took up a careful sight picture with his Desert Eagle. The second biker began squeezing off single shots from a pistol. Steve heard those rounds sailing by, wide of their mark. He squeezed off a single shot. That biker took the round in the chest and fell backward. The bike toppled with him.

The forest echoed with the first bike's engine as the rider faded from view. Steve broke from cover and raced up the hill toward the now idle dirt bike.

Below and to his left, the second suspect with the AK-47 still blazed away at A.J. and Shaver. Steve took the chance that the rifle was not aimed in his direction. Miano could take this guy.

The forest was suddenly rocked by the roar of the chopper as it swooped over the trees. Seconds later, it made another pass, circling the area as the pilot scoped things out.

Steve's heart and lungs pounded as he climbed at a run. Closing in on the downed bike, he spotted what appeared to be a shelter. It was crudely constructed of wood, with a roof and slat walls. Through what appeared to be a doorway, he could see bedding and some trash. He also observed numerous trash items strewn about the area.

Just up the hill, he reached the bike. The rider had crawled away and collapsed just a few feet behind the bike.

Steve ignored him for the moment. He picked up the bike and swung his leg over. He then fumbled with the controls, hand and foot. He'd ridden motorcycles before, but it had been awhile. He searched for where the gears were, all the while his escaping suspect putting more distance behind him—

Something suddenly collided with him, knocking him off the bike and to the forest floor. Apparently, the suspect he'd shot was not dead, or even incapacitated. Steve rolled off his shoulder and the Lazarus suspect sprawled next to him. He quickly rolled to his hands and knees and launched himself at the cop. Steve saw the knife in his hand.

Having risen to a knee, Steve found himself in a perfect position to thwart the attack. As the suspect leapt onto him, Steve allowed himself to roll backward. He grabbed an arm and planted his foot in the man's gut. He rolled backward toward the slope and launched with his leg.

The suspect flew off his boot and sailed down the slope. Steve soon heard how fortuitous his aim was. The man tumbled through the air, only to crash through the roof of the crude shelter they'd constructed. The roof collapsed, and he fell through, landing in the collapsing pile of chunks of lumber. Steve took a moment to check him from up the hill and he did not see the man stir.

Blazer returned to the motorcycle. He kicked the starter, and the bike squealed to life. He then kicked at the gear and twisted the accelerator handle. Mud spun from his tires as the bike took off.

Where am I going? Steve asked himself. He finally

got to examine the path in front of him and he found something of a trail worn into the green grass, leaves and pine needles. Whatever it was, it appeared to be crisscrossed by mud streaks where the bike tires kicked up the forest floor. Steve followed that trail.

Knowing his suspect had nearly two minutes lead, Steve poured on the speed. He could feel the bike engine racing beneath him and he stood in his seat, using his legs to cushion him from the rough ride. There were half buried rocks and tree roots in the trail worn into the forest floor. But then, that's probably what gave these guys the thrills as they rode these machines through here. He kept the throttle twisted full-on, kept the engine squealing. From the direction the trail went it appeared to head toward the access road they had just hiked from.

He followed the trail as it wound along the side of the canyon wall, slowly descending toward the road. After a minute of bouncing down the trail, he spotted his suspect ahead. He goosed an extra surge of power from the bike, and in another few seconds, he saw that he was closing the distance.

Just ahead, the trail swung around a dip in the hillside. The suspect followed the trail. The dip appeared harmless enough, just wet grass. Steve made a quick choice. He turned the bike and leapt it off the edge, rolling down into the land bowl. Like a rollercoaster, he flew up the other side, and into the air over the trail. He passed just behind the suspect and landed just off the trail to his left. Steve let the shocks absorb the landing but had to fight for a moment to maintain his balance.

The suspect glanced back at him, then goosed his throttle. Steve did the same, leaning right and swerving back onto the muddy trail.

He managed to bring himself side by side with the suspect. They rode like this for several tense seconds, both glancing repeatedly at the other, conjuring up their next move—

The suspect suddenly kicked out with his left leg. He missed Blazer, but hit the bike, knocking Steve sideways. Blazer leaned with the kick, regaining his balance. The kick caused him to veer briefly off the trail, and he recovered quickly, swerving back toward it. He once again fishtailed onto the trail, sidling up next to the suspect.

It worked for the bad guy, Steve thought. As he swung in, he kicked out with his right leg. His aim was accidentally perfect, striking the man's knee.

They had entered a clearing with a creek bed bisecting it. The creek bed was strewn with thousands of small rocks and some partially buried tree roots, with only a small trickle of water from the hillside. When Steve kicked, it threw the suspect off balance. The bike entered the field of rocks at too awkward an angle. The bike hit a rock and was bumped into the air, just a few inches. The wheels briefly bounced between rocks like a bucking bronco. The suspect was thrown by the first buck and sailed over the handlebars. His airborne body slapped into the side of a thick tree, and he landed in a heap next to it.

Steve gripped his brake handle and fishtailed the bike into a sideways skid. I was just getting the hang of this motorcycle thing, he thought. He jumped off the bike, letting it drop where it fell, and drew his Desert Eagle. He made his way over the rocks to where the suspect had fallen.

He found the man pushing up from the ground, trying to get back to his feet. Steve circled behind him and suddenly planted a foot in his back, forcing him back down to the ground. "Stay there," he said. "And by the way, you're under arrest."

The suspect collapsed under his foot, stunned from his crash. Steve knelt down, now planting a knee in his back. He holstered and drew handcuffs from the pouch at the back of his belt. "Can you walk?" he asked.

The man's response was to move both legs. Steve rolled him over to bring him up, but he paused, getting a better look at the man. He was shorter, topping five foot ten. His head was shaved, but his face sported a mustache and a long goatee. He wore a light jacket in the cold morning air, but it was open, exposing a wife-beater T-shirt below. Steve saw that he was heavily tattooed, visible under his shirt, as well as his neck, and a few designs on his face.

"Come on," Steve said, maneuvering him to his feet. He estimated it was less than half a mile back to the camp, and they began their hike.

Only now did he realize that gunfire back at the camp was still blazing.

* * *

A.J. glanced out from behind his tree to get a line on where the shooter was. The AK-47 rattled again as he exposed himself, but he ducked back behind the cover of the tree and the line of bullets stitched the dirt next to him. A.J. leaned out the other side of the tree and opened fire at the guy. Now he was pissed.

The shooter was standing in the open, and as the cop leaned out in front of him, he leveled the AK-47 in his direction.

A.J.'s first two rounds kicked up mud behind the shooter, but the man's chest suddenly spouted geysers of blood. Lots of them. He danced a final dance then collapsed onto wet grass.

A.J. detected movement on his right and swung his gun in that direction. Two men were approaching at a run. He lowered his weapon—Shaver's other two agents had made it back across the river.

A.J. was not about the leave his life in the hands of Shaver and his group. He suddenly burst from cover and ran, not for the fallen tree, but for the hillside to the right, the same path Blazer had taken would get him behind the ambush site. He felt the eyes of the DEA agents on him as he ran. He scaled the side of the little dip until he could just peak over the edge. He played his gun over the dip, and slowly stepped higher. He finally sat down and slid down the grassy hillside into the shadow of the fallen tree.

No other bad guys waited for him. "All clear!" he shouted.

He took a moment to examine the bunker that had been created there. It was pretty well stocked. He saw a couple of blankets, some bottles of water, and a dozen more magazines for the AK-47. These guys were ready for a fight. Steve was right, they had heard the chopper overhead and probably just assumed it would be law enforcement. They could have just as easily melted into the forest and disappeared. But they chose to fight.

A.J. ducked outside the bunker. Shaver had emerged from cover and was checking the dead machine gunner. He had moved the AK-47 away in case the man miraculously came back to life. A.J. exchanged a look with him. He half expected some kind of chastisement for his actions under fire, but Shaver said nothing to him.

Instead, Shaver turned to his men. "Watch this suspect," he said, "I want to get a look at the rest of this camp."

* * *

Considering what he'd seen of the suspect he'd captured; Steve wasn't taking any chances with the guy. His hands were cuffed behind his back, and they'd walked the entire distance back to the camp with Steve holding the chain to the cuffs. One wrong move and Steve could jerk them up and elicit some pain compliance. He could also simply throw the subject back to the ground.

As they approached the camp minutes later, Steve noticed that the AK-47 had gone silent. Steve considered calling Miano on his cell phone to check his status. He had his doubts about reception, so instead he bellowed, "Police! Hello the camp!"

"Blazer!" Miano shouted, "We're clear, come on in."

Steve pushed his suspect forward, following the muddied trail into the camp.

As they entered, Steve took in all the changes. Miano, Shaver and the other two DEA Agents had gathered at the camp. They had cuffed the man Steve had kicked through the roof of the shelter. He was alive but unconscious, now sitting against another fallen tree. Steve kicked his suspect's knees out from behind, sitting him down next to the unconscious man. The two agents had been tasked with guard duty.

"You alright, Sarge?" A.J. asked as Steve walked up.

"I'm good. This guy took a header in a creek bed. You?"

"Alive. Two shooters dead down the way. You called it—they were waiting for us."

Steve nodded and looked at Shaver. "Have you found what you're looking for?"

"And more. Come on, I'll show you."

They walked past the collapsed shanty. "Obviously, this was their living shelter," Shaver began. Steve got a look at the living conditions. The space was wide enough for all four men, with a flimsy wooden roof haphazardly nailed between two trees. Blue tarp had been removed and folded sloppily next to the shanty. Also inside, he saw wadded up clothing piled everywhere. Where there was not clothing, he saw food wrappers, anything from Styrofoam containers from Mexican restaurants to emptied tin cans, and even a pizza box. There were lots of beer cans and bottles laying around. Steve saw other food containers discarded all over the camp. The group had completely trashed the entire hillside.

Shaver pointed to something tucked against a tree trunk next to the shanty. "They had a generator at their disposal. This is what ran the water pump that drew from the river." Steve saw two electrical cords running from the generator, one to the shanty and to a small device against another nearby tree. The hose that drew from the river led up to the device and another hose stretched off in another direction.

Shaver led him further down the ridge, following that second hose. "The water pumped first to that field of young plants. When those young plants get big enough, they would be moved into the main field. The water gets pumped up there, too." He stopped and swept a hand in a flourish.

Steve had seen the field as they approached. Planted among the towering trees, he saw rows of a different green, hundreds of plants standing nearly six feet tall. At his feet, he noted an elaborate network of water hoses that branched off into every row of plants. Near a corner of the grow field, Steve saw a black tarp. Part of it had been pulled away by Shaver, and he saw piles of heavy white plastic bags underneath. The agent followed his gaze. "Fertilizer and pesticide. You remember the rat poison I told you about? Those two chemicals are literally poisoning this area. Then it gets into the drainage water, which finds its way to the creek. As we've seen, it doesn't just poison the fish and the wildlife."

Steve nodded toward a pile of plants that had been uprooted and laid out on another tarp. "Looks like they may have started harvesting."

"Could be. I'm getting some backup in here with us. We're going to start tearing the rest up so we can transport them by chopper to our facility for destruction."

Shaver led Steve back to the camp, where the others waited. "Now," he resumed, stopping over their suspects, "the question is, what do we do with these two?"

"That's going to have to be your department," Steve said.

"What do you mean?"

"You're the federal agent," Steve said. "Take a good look at your suspects. Notice their tattoos." Everyone glanced at the two Mexicans. They were finally able to get a look at the designs all over their bodies. Both sported ink on their arms and chest. But one, the suspect Steve had chased down, had tattoos all over his goateed face and shaved head. In particular, they noted the number thirteen painted next to both eyes. "These guys are straight out of the Mexican Mafia. That means they are mostly likely illegal aliens. Two months ago, California became a sanctuary state. That means, much as I'd like to, my partner and I could face repercussions if we do too much to them. I would also not recommend housing them in our county jail, or they will end up back on the streets with nothing but a notice to appear, wink wink, nudge nudge. Considering these guys just tried to kill cops, including you, I would do everything in my power to keep them in custody and away from San Francisco's judicial system."

"I see your point," Shaver said. "I can make arrangements."

"Whatever you do," Steve went on, "make sure you have warrants for absolutely everything you do in San Francisco. There are people in town looking to screw you any way they can. You know how crazy that city is."

CHAPTER 8

Kevin knew he couldn't avoid it anymore, he had to go to school today. He managed to wake up early, before the sun came up. He sat quietly by his window and smoked the last of the weed Randy had left him, debating whether to stop in the kitchen for breakfast. He decided he wasn't ready to confront his parents. They were just going to lecture him more on school, his grades, and the cops. He just needed to escape all that. He had enough problems with the football team wanting to kill him. He had Kevin's loaner to help him deal with them. He grabbed his backpack, complete with the gun inside, and stepped out of his room.

The house was dark and quiet. Parents must not be up yet, he thought. Typical, his dad was a bum and mom was not exactly Susie Homemaker. He headed for the front door, opened it quietly, and slipped outside.

He froze before closing the door. His dad sat on the front porch, staring into the fog. He raised a cigarette to his lips and took a long drag. It wasn't a tobacco cigarette, Kevin smelled the marijuana smoke around him.

His dad slowly turned to face him. "Off to school early, I see."

"Uh, yeah."

"Well, it can only help your grades. Do I need to call the cops to make sure you're there?"

"Come on, Dad, are you really going to ride me at seven in the morning?"

"Gotta start the day right." He took a quick puff. "Kevin, look at me. I'm forty years old, and my body is broken, and I can't work, which means I can't provide for you and your mom. I don't want you to end up like us."

This is the weirdest lecture I've ever gotten, Kevin thought. Could it be because he was listening to his stoned father while he himself was high? "Trust me, I don't want to end up like you."

"OK, good. Don't take after me, I'm a pathetic addict. But once you resolve to do better than me with your life, you need a plan. How are you going to do it?"

"Come on, Dad, are we going to do this now?"

"You gotta do it sometime. Figure out what you want out of your life. School is a start, but then what?"

Kevin suddenly blew up. "I don't know, alright? I don't know what I'm going to do. I don't know what I want out of my life. I damn sure don't want to work some bullshit dead-end job for the rest of my life. I damn sure don't want to end up like you, trapped in a loveless marriage with a kid like me."

His dad stabbed out his joint and massaged a sudden ache in his left arm. He grimaced at that ache. "That's what you don't want. How about what you do want?"

"You never listen to me," Kevin shouted. "I just said I don't know!"

The door suddenly was yanked open from inside. His mom stood in the doorway, wearing a gray sweat suit as pajamas. "Hey," she shouted. "Would you two shut the hell up? Why are you arguing at the butt-crack of dawn anyway?"

"Just trying to give the boy some direction, Nora."

She threw up her hands in a 'whatever' gesture, retreated back inside and slammed the door.

"Now you've gone and woken up your mother," Ted said.

"I don't care!" Kevin shouted. "Neither one of you listen to me or know a thing about me. I'm sick of this!"

"Keep your voice down," Ted whispered, his voice suddenly sounding weak, strained.

"No, I'm sick of you guys! All you do is ride me about stupid shit!"

"I'm trying to tell you son," Ted said, rising shakily to his feet, "everything we're saying…it's for your own…"

He trailed off, then let out a gasp. He grabbed at his left arm, and suddenly dropped to his knees. He grunted and let out an agonized growl. He keeled over to his right and slumped onto the stoop.

"Dad?" Kevin's anger drained away, seeing his dad hit the porch this way. "Mom!" he shouted as he dropped to his knees. He began shaking his Dad, willing him to open his eyes. "Mom!" he shouted again.

His mom stuck her head outside again. "I told you to be—." She saw her husband collapsed. "Ted? Ted? Kevin, what did you do?"

"He just keeled over. Mom, wake him up!"

"Ted? Kevin, is he breathing?"

"I don't know. Do you know CPR?"

"I don't know CPR!" She stepped up to the railing. "Help! Help me!"

Some of their neighbors had finally stepped from their homes nearby, wanting to brave the commotion to come outside and start their day. Now that the commotion appeared to be a real emergency, some of those neighbors ventured forth to investigate. Nora never really paid too much attention to their neighbors; Ted was always the neighborly one. But she knew Wilton, the older Jewish retiree and Titus, the young black IT guy from across the street. They both came running when they saw Ted collapsed on their porch. Wilton's wife came out with their toy dog as well, and she trailed behind her husband, on the phone to 911.

Wilton and Titus jumped in like a heroic machine and began CPR. Wilton quickly breathed in two rescue breaths. Titus grabbed Ted's wrist. "I'm not feeling a pulse." He put his hands together on Ted's chest and began pushing

Kevin was practically shoved out of the way. Nora grabbed him, and they both watched in horror as the two men worked on Ted. Kevin had spent the last few weeks and months running away from everything his parents tried feebly to teach him. His headlong dive into marijuana was simply an escape, but Randy had made it seem almost like a way of life. But this was real life, slapping him in the face. What Titus had just said seemed to set the stage. No pulse. His dad was dying right in front of him. None of them could escape that.

Something else just said suddenly haunted him. His mom—she stood next to him, hugging her arms to her chest—she had asked…what did you do? She was blaming him for this. Considering all the shit Ted put in his body, he was probably the biggest offender when it came to damaging himself. But he had said some pretty bad things to his dad.

The CPR continued. "Still not getting a pulse," Wilton reported between rescue breaths.

He's gone, Kevin thought. And maybe I *am* to blame.

He suddenly couldn't deal with any of it. He needed to escape.

Before anyone could stop him, Kevin suddenly ran. He brushed past the neighbors trying to revive his dad. His mom called out to him, but her cries were lost among the voices of those working on Ted. He ran up the street and disappeared.

* * *

Scot Black and Dave Castillo reached the Haight around eight a.m. They knew that Green Resolve did not open for business until nine, so they scouted the area for a few minutes. The shop sat at the corner of Oak and Baker Streets and had several slanted parking spaces on the street in front of the shop. The intersection was right at the tip of the panhandle, the strip of grass and trees leading up to the eastern edge of Golden Gate Park. Scot managed to find a parking space on the street less than a block north on Baker. Dave was still recovering from his fight with Lynell Richards—he did not have a concussion, according to the doctor, but his head was still pounding. Scot left him in the vehicle to go conduct a quick reconnaissance.

Scot walked along the tip of the panhandle and crossed Oak, a one-way east bound street. He scoped out the surrounding area. Was anyone else doing their own surveillance, maybe casing the place? No suspicious persons or vehicles stood out. He did notice an abundance of homeless people around. In the grass of the park, he saw dozens of transients camped out, bundled against the morning cold. Ironically, once he crossed Oak, he saw no homeless people camped in front of the dispensary.

Scot stopped casually at the corner, near the front door. He once again searched for anyone watching him, then slipped up to the front door and gave it a quick examination. He was looking for scrapes in the wood, a broken latch, anything that would indicate that the place had already been burglarized. It looked clear and secured. He broke away and walked down the block. A small alley opened up here, and he walked through. The shop had a back door here, and he checked the door and windows for any sign of burglary, finding none.

Minutes later, he returned to their unmarked vehicle. Dave had been watching his progress, and Scot reported to him that the business was secure. They settled into what they hoped—and feared—would be a fruitless surveillance.

The first two hours of the stakeout dragged by. Dave dozed a bit in the passenger seat. He was under doctor's orders to "take it easy," so Scot was ok with him napping. In fact, Black was taking it upon himself to watch his partner and make sure he was OK.

Around eleven a.m., Dave suddenly shook himself awake. "How long was I out?"

"You've been in and out for the last hour."

"Damn. I'm sorry, bro."

"It's all good."

"No, I'm supposed to be carrying my own weight here. I can participate in a stakeout."

Scot smiled. "You're doing a great job so far." He glanced at his partner. "You're under doctor's orders. Dr. Black says relax. Enjoy the down time."

Scot remained intent on the shop, the sparse crowds passing it by, as well as those going in. "It's weird, and at the same time typical. This place has been open for two hours. Every single customer I've seen go in there has been young and male. I have not seen one granny go in for her glaucoma meds. I've seen a lot of these panhandle-camping transients wake up and go straight inside." Scot watched a vehicle pull up and park in one of the slanted spaces on Baker Street. It was another thug-mobile, a brightly painted muscle car. He suddenly burst out laughing. "You know what else I've noticed? That first parking space on the corner is a Handicap space. I haven't seen one car park there."

Dave smiled at the observation. "They're all lying about their chronic pain and everybody's got a guilty conscience."

Scot suddenly perked up. "Two guys in hoodies crossing Baker," he reported to his partner.

Dave grabbed the pair of binoculars before Scot could. If this was the guy who assaulted him last night, he wanted a piece of him. He trained the binos on the two crossing Baker Street. If they were headed into the dispensary, he had only seconds to identify them. "Gray hoodies," he reported. "Both have solid builds...wearing gloves...Can't see any skin, can't tell race..."

The larger of the two mounted the step and entered the shop. His partner stopped for a moment outside to survey the street. Dave finally got a look at his face. "This one is an adult male, black. I don't recognize him." The subject then turned and went inside. "Shit, they could be starting their robbery right now."

"We don't have enough yet," Scot said.

"Come on, Black, we have enough for a recon. One or both of us could go in and see what they're up to. If they're just customers, we stand down. If they're doing anything else, we take care of business."

Scot was convinced. "OK. You gonna make it?"

"I'm fine. Let's go!"

They bolted from the vehicle. Neither drew a weapon just yet, as they did not know what they were dealing with. As they ran along the trees lining the street, both had their eyes locked on the front door.

When they reached the corner, Scot motioned to Dave, and they started to circle toward the west. Scot checked Oak Street, seeking cover somewhere near the front door. He thought he saw movement through a window in the door, and he didn't want to be seen just yet—

He was too late. The front door suddenly flew open. One man in a hoodie stepped out. He raised a gun and fired.

The street was wide open. Traffic was stopped at a light just down Oak Street. A few nearby pedestrians reacted. Women screamed at the sudden shots. Men ducked for cover and dragged the women with them.

Both cops scrambled for cover behind a row of newspaper vending machines, with Scot at one end and Dave at the other. They felt the bullets impact the machines, the *plink* of each impact audible over the shots.

Scot positioned himself on his knee. He suddenly raised up over the machines. In that moment, he saw no other risk and loosed a quick volley of shots.

The suspect ducked forward behind a parked car and fired again. At least one round threw sparks from a paper machine right next to Black. As he ducked down, Dave rose at the other end. He rapid fired an entire magazine. He ducked down as his magazine ran dry. A heartbeat later, bullets punched at the metal next to him.

With Castillo drawing the fire, Scot rose again. He drew a bead on the car. The shooter was ducked behind it, but Scot had a clear shot at—

He fired a double tap. His rounds punched through the front windows, shattering the glass. Beyond them, he saw the suspect convulse and collapse.

He didn't notice that the traffic light a block away had turned green, and the line of cars began to advance, apparently unaware of the gunfire crossing their path.

He did notice the second suspect suddenly coming out the door. The man opened up on Scot's end of the vending machines. Scot ducked down, just as he saw the suspect begin to run, west bound on Oak.

"He's on the run!" Scot announced to Dave. Scot rose and ran after the suspect, for the moment staying on the north side of Oak.

That suspect was suddenly lost behind the line of traffic.

Scot strained to watch him beyond the passing cars. But he didn't see the suspect suddenly open fire again.

He'd seen a break in traffic, with an Acura SUV racing ahead of the vehicles behind it. As it neared the suspect, he raised his gun and began to pepper the vehicle's front end with bullets. The SUV suddenly swerved. The right front tire blew, and that, plus the driver trying to avoid the gunfire, caused the SUV to lose control. The SUV suddenly swerved left, then back to the right, until it plowed into a sedan parked at the corner, the one with the windows already shattered by gunfire. The SUV bounced backward out of the crash, now slamming almost broadside into a Toyota. That driver could not avoid the crash. The third driver in the Prius could not stop in time to avoid hitting the SUV now sitting across the lane before them. The Prius T-boned into the SUV. Behind the Prius, an eager motorcyclist had been trying to split lanes. He couldn't stop in time and laid his bike down. Motorcycle and rider separated as the bike slid ahead of him. The rider rolled to a stop. The bike slid up to the curb.

The suspect stepped out into the street. He picked up the motorcycle and swung his legs over. He twisted the throttle. The rear wheel spun, the friction burning off blue-black smoke. Then the tire gripped, and he rocketed forward.

Scot had been distracted by the traffic collision, watching to make sure drivers would be OK. The motorcycle shot across the street right in front of him. The suspect riding it lifted his handlebars and the bike jumped the curb, riding into the panhandle.

Scot turned back to Dave. "One suspect is down, secure this crime scene." As Dave nodded, Scot turned and raced off after the motorcycle on foot.

Dave crossed the street through the stopped vehicles. He mounted the opposite sidewalk with his gun trained on their downed suspect. He approached quickly but watched for any sign that the guy was alive and waiting to ambush him. Dave saw the automatic still clutched in his hand. He stepped on that hand to immobilize the gun where it was and elicit a response from a live suspect. There was no response. He pushed with his foot, removing the gun from the suspect's hands and shifting it away. He holstered and knelt over the guy, feeling his wrist for a pulse. Considering the growing pile of blood under his torso, he was not surprised to find no pulse. Just up the street, people were coming out of other businesses, ready to offer their help. Dave motioned to them. "Police, stay back."

One man nodded and then bolted out into the street to begin assisting those involved in the crash.

Dave stood up, surveying the crashed cars as he pulled out his cell phone. "This is Inspector Castillo." He gave his badge number and location. "I need fire and EMS, multiple ambulances, to my location. I've got a serious traffic collision, looks like four cars involved. I'll be checking for injuries. Also, I need a few black-and-whites to direct traffic and secure a crime scene." He hung up and plunged into the street and rushed to the first car to check the driver's condition.

* * *

As Scot raced through the trees north across the panhandle, he wondered how he was going to keep up with the motorcycle on foot. He could still hear the engine, but the bike had turned west through the trees of the panhandle, and he briefly lost sight of it.

A possible answer suddenly presented itself. He heard a strange thundering noise, something slapping concrete. As he cleared the trees onto Fell Street, he spotted the motorcycle racing west bound on Fell and veering into the park.

He then observed two horses galloping in his direction.

Mounted police patrolling Golden Gate Park.

Scot quickly fished out his badge and steered toward the horse cops. They saw him and reined in their steeds.

"Inspector Black. I need to pursue that motorcycle."

Both mounted officers glanced over at the motorcycle, which had steered onto John F Kennedy Drive. "Climb on board," one officer said. To his partner, he said, "Go check out that accident." He reached down, and Scot grabbed his arm. He was inexperienced around horses, but he knew that mounted officers waited years for a slot on the exclusive detail and won many awards at shows around the country. They were very skilled at what they did. Scot was hoisted onto the horse's back behind the rider.

Before the second rider departed, Black called out, "My partner is over there, we have one suspect down. He could use the assist." In an instant, the mounted cop spurred his horse and Scot found himself bouncing along after the retreating motorcycle.

Scot was lost on how to behave on the horse. For a moment, he felt like he was going to slide right off. He reached forward and grabbed onto the officer's duty belt while trying to situate himself at the back of the saddle. He then bent his knees and used them as a platform draped over the horse to keep him from bouncing too hard and sliding off. The horse took to a canter down JFK Drive. Several cars slowed down as the horse galloped into the street, his shoes *clopping* hard on the pavement.

The motorcycle rider must have heard something. He glanced behind and did a visible double take, seeing the horse racing after him. He then veered right, toward the nearest building, the Conservatory of Flowers. He jumped the bike onto the grass there, steering around a few sparse clusters of tourists. Scot saw the motorcycle's rear wheel tearing the grass up, kicking clumps into the air behind him. The horse galloped noisily after him. The noise diminished once the horse was galloping across the grass.

Despite the pursuit, Scot could see the motorcycle gaining ground. "Can't this ride go any faster?"

The Mountie cocked his head toward him. "I'm sorry, Inspector. If I go any faster, you're going to fly right off."

The motorcycle rider raced up a slight hill at the west side of the Conservatory. The motorcycle engine gunned, and Scot saw him fly into the air at the crest of the small hill. He flew between two trees and disappeared.

"Keep going!" Scot urged his equestrian partner.

They reached the hill seconds later, and saw that beyond a small copse of trees, the park opened up to a meadow. Riding through, Scot saw marks in the grass where the bike had gone, but the bike had disappeared. He couldn't even hear the motor anymore. "Keep going," he said again, feeling more and more like it was a futile gesture.

The mounted cop took it upon himself to try and follow the tracks in the grass. In moments, they were within sight of Fulton Street, the northern barrier of Golden Gate Park.

Scot suddenly perked up, seeing a vehicle speeding along Fulton. The familiar Chrysler 300 drove past them. Scot heard that engine suddenly roar as the driver spotted the horse in the park. The Chrysler sped away. There was no chance of catching the car, but this was the confirmation Scot needed. He had no doubt now that their suspect was Lynell Richards.

"We can slow down now," he told the mounted cop. "That was our suspect."

The rider brought the heavily panting horse down to a walk. Moments later, they came across the motorcycle, dropped and abandoned at the edge of the park.

"Wait here," Scot directed his equestrian partner. The mounted cop *whoaed* the horse and Scot gracelessly jumped from the back. He ran up to the bike and circled it once but did not touch it. He fished out his cell phone and called dispatch. "This is Inspector Black, SFPD," he announced. He gave his badge number as he searched for a nearby road sign. "I need a sector car to 8th and Fulton."

When he hung up with dispatch, Scot took a moment to walk around the bike one more time and scan it visually for anything that might be useful to the investigation. CSI could check for the usual, fingerprints, hair, fibers. Since their suspect was wearing gloves, finding anything was unlikely. But… "This bike is part of the crime scene," he said to the equestrian cop. Before he could go on, a squad car pulled up to the sidewalk, its blue lights blinking. A single officer stepped out, and Scot badged him. "Inspector Black, Special Forces. You've heard about the accident scene by the panhandle?"

"Yeah, I got diverted from there."

Scot pointed. "This bike is part of that crime, dumped by a 211 suspect. I need you to watch it until CSI comes for it."

The officer briefly seemed surprised by the assignment, but said, "OK."

Scot hurried back to the horse. He felt like an old pro now as the mounted cop pulled him back up. He turned his steed and they took off at a slower canter.

They steered well clear of the Conservatory of Flowers to minimize any damage to the grounds. As they rode toward the panhandle, Scot could hear sirens approaching. When they reached Oak Street, he could see the activity ahead. A fire truck and two ambulances were at the end of the block. One block west of the scene, the horse cop's partner was guiding traffic down Lyon Street, away from the crash. He reined in at that intersection. Scot swung off the back of the horse, fumbling through another awkward dismount. "Thanks for the ride."

"Someday you'll have to tell me the story of just what happened here," the Mountie said.

"One day, I'm sure I will." Scot turned and ran off in search of his partner.

Other uniforms had already put up crime scene tape and crowds were already gathering outside. Some of the neighboring merchants had come out to help victims of the crash, making themselves part of the scene. Scot badged a uniform and was allowed to duck underneath the tape. He found Dave assisting paramedics as they moved a woman out of the vehicle that had T-boned the shot-up SUV. Paramedics eased the woman onto a backboard and began to fix a plastic collar brace around her neck. Once she was secured, Scot stepped back so paramedics could work on her and take her to an ambulance.

Scot joined his partner. "What your status?"

"Suspect is DOA, I've got him secured where he fell." He nodded toward a single uniform on the sidewalk. The body was behind the parked car, out of sight from the public. "His gun has been photographed, collected and secured as well. As for the crash, it's mostly minor injuries. No one hit by gunfire.

"Good."

Dave looked pointedly at him. "I take it our second suspect got away."

"Hey, nothing I could do. But I am almost certain it was Lynell Richards. His Chrysler 300 was parked nearby. I saw that vehicle fleeing." He turned toward the front door of Green Resolve. "Have you been inside yet?"

"I was waiting for you."

Scot led them up to the door, and en route cast a quick glance over the downed suspect. He pushed open the door. A cheery bell was triggered by the door as they entered. They were confronted by a set up similar to the other dispensaries they'd seen recently. Somewhat dim lighting, with shelves full of product. Only one glass pane had been shattered, and that particular shelf was free of any product. It appeared that their armed robbers had not had the chance to steal much.

They came face to face with three Hispanic males standing behind the counter. Two were dressed casually, jeans and black T-shirts. The third was dressed nicer, in jeans, a dark gray button down short and tie, partially covered by a leather jacket. He sported a devilish goatee and a handful of small tattoos were visible on his neck. They appeared to be engaged in a whispered conversation, and the exchange cut off as the cops walked in.

Scot's eyes swept over the group. "Is everybody OK?"

One of the casual dressers stepped forward, came

out from behind the counter. "Yeah, man," he said with a thick accent. "We're OK. Nobody injure."

"I'm Inspector Black, this is Inspector Castillo. Can you tell us what happened?"

The speaker seemed unsure of himself, and to Scot, it struck him as more than just a language barrier. One thought surfaced, that these guys might be illegal aliens. It didn't matter as California had just become a sanctuary state, and he was forbidden by law from asking their immigration status or pursuing any action regarding it. But he really was only interested in the crime at hand.

"These two guys, they come in, they pull guns. One says he wants all the weed. But we didn't really have time to get anything for them, just stuff from there. The other guy, he sees cops outside, so they go out shooting."

As he listened, Dave was to one side, looking at the shelves. He found one shelf that had a display of edibles, including a variety of candy bars. Every single one had a wrapper that mimicked a popular candy bar, from Kit Kat to Hershey to Reese's. He could see kids mistaking these for the real thing at home and eating it. The next shelf over had baggies of green bud, and each had a label. They had cheery names, such as Green Crack, Flava Fuel, Cookie Kush, Green Ghost...and he came upon a prominent display with a bright sign proudly boasting of the Green Resolve signature flavor, Revolution Reefer. Dave couldn't help but shake his head. All to minimize the stigma of smoking dope and even to fight the power and support the legalization revolution.

"OK," Scot said. "I want to get a more detailed statement from you guys. Can I ask you to step outside with me? We're considering this a crime scene now."

He led the three of them outside to the chaos. Scot

waved over a uniformed officer. "This officer will stay with you and we'll speak with you shortly." He did not wait for a reaction from the men. He grabbed Dave, and they went back toward the shop.

Behind them, they did not see the staff members exchange a worried look. One nodded to the well-dressed man who nodded back. He casually watched the officer babysitting them. That officer leaned into his vehicle to check something on his data terminal. Seeing his opportunity, the well-dressed man slipped away, ducking under the yellow tape nearby.

One of the ambulances was leaving. Scot stopped at the door and pulled his cell phone. "Something isn't right in there," he said to his partner. "I can't put my finger on it, but…" He first dialed Captain Stanson. "Cap, it's Inspector Black. I don't know if you've heard yet, we have a major incident going down by the Golden Gate Park Panhandle. One suspect DOA outside the dispensary Blazer has had his eye on. Copy, see you shortly."

Scot hung up, and Dave saw him tapping his phone again. "The Sarge needs to know what's going on and we're going to need to find Lynell. I'm calling Blazer."

CHAPTER 9

Once things had calmed down at the marijuana grow, Steve took it upon himself to scout the forest around the camp site. He wanted to make sure there were no further threats, no other Mexican Mafia soldiers lurking and waiting for their opportunity for one final strike. While he searched, Shaver made a call to his DEA office. Back up was summoned and crews were requested to come and help chop down the plants to haul them off for destruction. When Steve returned from his reconnaissance, he eagerly grabbed a pick from among a stash of gardening tools at the camp. He began attacking the plants himself. The others looked on as he did so, wondering what was driving him. Even A.J. still wondered sometimes what was behind Blazer's rage against drugs.

Shaver's backup crews were already on standby and they arrived in less than an hour. The echoes of helicopters permeated the forest as those choppers landed at the designated spot on the access road. By this time, with A.J. helping, Steve had made a significant dent in chopping down plants. Minutes later, crews arrived on foot, guided in by one of

Shaver's DEA partners. Shaver gave instructions to the work crews and they dispersed to their duties. Some trekked up the hill to begin tearing down the camp and cleaning up the trash. Others joined the SFPD cops in chopping down plants.

Steve picked up a stalk he had just felled and dragged it down to a pile he had made. One of the DEA agents spread out a large white canvas, and Steve recognized what it was. The plants would be piled up on it and it would wrap them up to be airlifted out by chopper. He dragged this plant to the canvas and tossed it on, then began dragging the rest of the pile toward the canvas.

Steve paused to take a breath. He again caught a whiff of the smell of marijuana. He'd always hated that smell. He looked at his gloves, which were coated with green resin from the plants and reeked of weed. "I'm going to have to get rid of these gloves," he remarked to A.J., who was working nearby.

Blazer's cell phone suddenly vibrated, and he ripped off the gloves, thankful for the chance to do so. He fished the phone out of a pocket on his BDU pants. Caller ID showed Scot's name on the screen. "Blazer."

"It's Black. Lynell just tried to hit Green Resolve. He and his partner shot at us and caused a major car wreck on the street. Partner is DOA, but Lynell is in the wind."

"Damn," Steve breathed. "OK, we're coming back. I want this guy off the street if he's becoming that dangerous."

"Captain's on the way. We'll be here working the crime scene for a while. Get here quick." Scot hung up.

Steve slipped his phone back in his pocket and motioned to Miano. A.J. had heard Steve's end of the call. Steve dropped his pick and hurried down the ridge with A.J. on his heels.

"Shaver!" Steve approached the DEA agent. "We have to get back to the city. Our suspect just hit Green Resolve and tried to rob it. We have to find him and stop his crime wave."

"Damn it," Shaver said. "That means I have to move up my timetable. I have plans in the works to shut the place down and dig into its books. I think we should do that now."

Steve suddenly smiled. "If you need warrants, I know a judge we can talk to."

"OK. Let's head down to the access road. I'll call the chopper."

The easiest way for them to get back was to return to the river and follow it down to the access road. The trek took fifteen minutes. Steve walked deep in thought, laying out in his mind everything he knew about their suspect, Richards, the status of the case against him, and how everything seemed to center on this one pot dispensary. Scot hadn't given him too much detail about their incident, but he seemed confident that Lynell Richards was behind it. Steve wanted an airtight case to prove it.

They reached the road and climbed up a rocky embankment to the pavement. Steve saw that DEA Agents had been busy here. There were several un-marked law enforcement vehicles, Ford Explorers and Crown Victorias. It appeared they had shut down the road.

Steve stopped on the road, suddenly not knowing where he should go.

Shaver was the last to make the climb from the river. He was involved in a push-to-talk conver-sation on his phone that ended with a "Roger." He approached Blazer and Miano. "The chopper was farther away than I hoped. They'll be here in ten minutes."

Steve nodded, and once again retreated into his thoughts.

Movement to his left drew his attention, and he glanced down the road. A vehicle drifted slowly around the bend but stopped suddenly. Steve made out the shape of a white van. He watched it for a second. Two deputies borrowed from the county sheriff's office for the detail were conversing at their vehicles and did not see the van. The vehicle backed away around the corner and disappeared.

Something struck him as odd. It did not appear that the van was a law enforcement vehicle or they wouldn't have retreated. Was it possibly connected to the grow?

"Shaver," he beckoned the agent. "Are you expecting any more personnel here?"

"No, just the chopper. Why?"

"I just saw a van turn the corner down there. They backed away and took off." Steve hurried toward the deputies, who still were engaged in a conversation with each other. "Hey, guys, did you see that van?" Steve knew the answer, and the blank looks were not a surprise. "Can I get one of you to head down that way toward the highway and try to find it? Check it out and get word back to us here what you find." The deputies exchanged a look and one opened his patrol car door. He backed away and started down the road.

Minutes dragged by, until the sounds of a helicopter rotor once again filtered into the area. Steve walked back to the deputy. "Any word?"

"He just radioed back, sir. He's driven several miles down and he's found no sign of the vehicle."

"OK, thanks." Steve suspected he knew what had happened. Once they were out of sight of the law enforcement, they probably floored it to escape the area, or maybe had another hidey hole somewhere to take cover in. Steve rejoined his partner. The chopper settled in over them and drifted downward. Steve shielded his face—the ground was moist from recent rains, but some dust was still kicked up by rotor-wash. Once the Jayhawk settled to the hardtop, Steve let Shaver be the first to approach. He and A.J. followed, and they boarded.

Before he belted in, Steve reached for an intercom headset. Shaver donned his as well. "We need to follow the road back to the highway," he announced to the pilot. "Keep your eyes open for a white van." The pilot glanced back at him, and then nodded. They lifted off one minute later.

He couldn't shake his suspicions about the van. His hopes for finding it dwindled, but there was something about it. He thought over what he knew about the grow, and how Shaver was trying to tie it to Green Resolve. He thought back to his surveillance of the dispensary. He swore he remembered seeing a van like that in the parking section on the street. But was he remembering it simply because he *wanted* to tie it to the dispensary? And what about the van seen by all the neighbors at the first grow house they had busted?

They followed the road back toward the edge of the National Forest and no one saw any sign of the van. Everyone shrugged at Steve, and he shrugged right back at them. He settled back for the trip back to the bay and Yerba Buena Island.

* * *

Steve chafed at the delay as the chopper slowly settled onto the island. Once he and the others were out, the chopper lifted off again to return to duty at the National Forest. There, it would resume hunting for more grow sites. As the wind and the noise died down, Steve led them toward the fence surrounding the airfield, beyond which lay their vehicles.

"I'll head to the DEA office and get the ball rolling," Shaver said. "I'm shutting that dispensary down. Go make sure your people are OK and go find this suspect."

"Thanks," Steve said pushing through the gate. His black SUV was parked right there and he used a remote to unlock it.

Shaver reached his own unmarked Crown Victoria. "And text me that Judge's name and number."

"You got it." Steve and A.J. climbed into his SUV.

Steve maneuvered his SUV through a couple of windy streets, seeking the road that climbed toward Interstate 80 and the Bay Bridge. A.J. took it upon himself to text Shaver the information he needed.

Steve headed for the dispensary, which was all the way across town. He stayed on 80 across the bridge and followed it south through the city until Highway 101 branched off to the west. When he exited the freeway there, he was just blocks from the Panhandle.

Steve got a look at the scene as he pulled to the side of Oak Street at the tip of the panhandle. There were police vehicles, marked and unmarked, up and down the street and blocking the intersection. A tow truck was loading the last of the vehicles involved in the crash, and Steve saw the debris field of shattered glass and pieces of plastic scattered across the intersection. A CSI team was already on site taking pictures and sketches. With the damaged vehicles removed, Steve saw the covered body of the armed robber on the sidewalk in front of the pot shop.

Steve and A.J. were admitted into the crime scene by a uniform blocking the street. They found Scot and Dave standing at the corner and Captain Stanson was with them. Nearby, Steve recognized Saul Avery, his old partner in Homicide, conferring with a CSI photographer. Avery approached the group as well.

Steve glanced over his men, especially Dave, who had just been in the hospital. "You guys OK?"

"Yeah," Scot assured him. He briefed the Sergeant on the incident, from the two in hoodies entering, to the suspects coming out with guns blazing, to the one they believed was Lynell Richards shooting at a vehicle and causing the crash. Scot then nodded toward the mounted cops, still manning the traffic blockade down Oak Street, and described his chase on horseback.

"We've got plenty of circumstantial evidence against Lynell," he concluded. "I saw what I believe was his car fleeing the scene. We have a tentative ID on his dead partner here and he is a known associate."

"Did we ever figure out Lynell's parole status?" Steve asked.

"Oh, yeah," Dave said, "he's searchable. With the amount of weed he had when we arrested him the other day, he should have been violated."

Steve rolled his eyes. "Yeah, we all know what happened there. Let's talk to our store employees."

Scot nodded toward the patrol vehicle where he'd taken the three. As they approached, Scot muttered, "Something's wrong." Only two store employees were leaning against the back of the police Ford Crown Victoria. "Where's your friend?"

The men would only shake their heads.

Steve and Scot exchanged a glance. Something fishy was going on.

They stepped away for a moment, and Steve pulled out his cell phone. He dialed the number Shaver had given him, but instead of calling it, he sent a quick text: Where are you?

Steve beckoned Avery over. To the shop employees, he said, "This Inspector will take your statements."

Scot drew Blazer aside. "There was a third guy inside earlier, male Hispanic, thirties, well dressed, shirt and tie with a leather jacket, dark goatee, and a couple of tattoos."

Steve thought back to his motorcycle chase, and the man with the tatted face and chest. "Some things are coming together." His phone finally vibrated as Shaver answered his text, and Steve read, En route to SFPD HQ.

"Boss, I'm definitely itching to find this guy Lynell," Dave said.

Stanson approached in time to hear this. "I want him in custody, too. I want to know for sure if he did this, so we need to talk to him. Avery will run this crime scene and he can get statements from you two later today. I'm authorizing Special Forces to go find this guy."

Steve backed away from the group. "My guys, let's go." He pointed to Stanson and added, "We'll be in touch."

As they hurried to the vehicles, Steve took a moment to text Shaver back, "Meet me in lobby, have some questions." As they reached the vehicles, Steve said, "Scot, ride with me. A.J., first stop is Mission Rock lobby."

As they got under way, Scot said to Blazer, "How was your morning?"

* * *

The drive took an eternal fifteen minutes. Steve chafed at not being able to use his lights and sirens just to get through the traffic, moderate as it was. But he and Scot used the time to brief each other on events in their respective operations. He knew Dave and A.J. were doing the same. Among the four of them in two separate cars, it was like swapping war stories. Steve concluded his with, "You described a well-dressed guy with some tattoos. I'm hoping maybe Shaver can help us identify him. The guy I chased down was straight out of the Mexican mafia."

Steve parked his vehicle in the large parking lot as close to the building as he could, and A.J. parked nearby. As a team, they jogged out to the street and to the main entrance of the Mission Rock building.

Their timing was perfect. They found Agent Shaver at the center of an entourage standing in the lobby, several yards away from the front desk station. Shaver, still wearing his dirty camouflage pants and brown shirt, was surrounded by other DEA agents in suits. Standing next to him was an older man wearing slacks and polo shirt. Steve immediately recognized him. "Judge Allen, it's good to see you again, sir. Thank you for helping us on this."

"Sergeant Blazer, you're doing the Lord's work." Steve felt like the judge's smile was luck and a higher power smiling down on him.

He turned to Shaver. "You told me you had surveillance set up for a while at Green Resolve. Please tell me you have some kind of immediate access to photos, video, something."

Shaver smiled and took out his smart phone. He tapped the screen twice, then handed the phone over. "Just start scrolling."

He handed the phone toward Blazer, but Black grabbed it. He flicked his finger across the phone to begin his search.

Steve didn't hear the elevator chime ring behind him, but suddenly someone shouted, "Sergeant Blazer!"

The entire group turned to the new voice. Assistant District Attorney Kline had stepped off the elevator and now barreled toward the group. The short ADA walked right up to Blazer. "What are you doing to this town? What was this shootout by the Park?"

Steve narrowed his eyebrows. "I wasn't even there."

"Three people injured in a car accident…"

Steve nodded along with the story. "Caused by an armed felon committing a robbery."

"And all over a marijuana dispensary. This vendetta of yours has got to stop. This department is creating violence and destruction. And all for a substance that never killed anyone."

The older man with Shaver took a step forward. "Who is this person?" he asked Blazer.

"I'm Assistant District Attorney Kline," the weasely DA said, his tone becoming even more testy. "Who are you?"

"I'm Judge Allen." Steve watched Kline deflate a bit, and he enjoyed the sight. "I take it from your tone and rhetoric that you believe the police department is wrong for trying to stop the crime associated with the marijuana industry. Listen to me, young man. The voters have seen fit to legalize this 'substance,' as you call it, and that's fine. But there are plenty of other issues to go with it. There will be rules and law when it comes to legalized marijuana and the police are going to be tasked with seeing that those rules are followed. Otherwise, there will simply chaos on the street, I'm sure you would agree. We *want* the police to stop that chaos, I'm sure you would agree with that too. I've been watching this issue and this department a long time. Sergeant Blazer seems to be the first cop in a long time to actually be doing something about that chaos. I'm sure the DA's office will want to back him up in that fight. Would that be correct, ADA Kline?"

Every word seemed to deflate the weasel a little more. "Of course, your honor."

"Good. I'm sure Sergeant Blazer will contact someone in your department when a case is put together regarding the armed robbery that the police actually thwarted today. Thank you, Mr. Kline."

Kline had gone from deflating to actually looking like he'd been slapped in the face. He simply nodded, backed away and hurried out the front door.

Steve allowed himself a chuckle. He glanced at Allen. "Thanks, Judge."

The old man winked at him.

"This guy," Scot said behind them, and Steve hurried to his side. He got a look at the picture. It was a side shot of the man entering the shop, but Steve saw the right half of his mustache and goatee. "That's the guy that disappeared from Green Resolve."

Shaver took his phone back and glanced at the picture. "Yeah, we've identified him. His name is Diego Viejo. He's actually an enforcer and hit man for the Sureños gang we're looking at. Mexican police have connected him to a dozen murders, but of course they refuse to try and prove anything."

"He may pop up again," Steve said. "What's your status?"

"We're here to do affidavits and warrants. We should be headed to the dispensary within the hour."

"OK. I'll call Inspector Avery and have him detain those two employees for further questioning. Remember, we still have a crime scene active there. But I want to be there when you shut the place down. I'm hoping to have Richards in custody by then." Steve nodded, and he and his people turned and fled out the door. On the street, they ran back to the parking lot. As they reached their vehicles, Steve announced, "Next stop, the girlfriend's place."

* * *

Steve stopped his vehicle on the street a block away from Loqueesha's apartment. He quickly dialed Dave's cell phone and put his on speaker, so everyone in both cars could hear.

"We're not taking any more chances with this guy. I'm going in and going in hard. Scot, I want you on the fire escape, the floor above. He's not getting out that way. A.J., while we're getting into position, I want you to do a vehicle sweep of the surrounding streets and see if you can spot his Chrysler 300. Report if you find it. Then position yourself in the alley below the fire escape. Dave, you're with me. Let's move."

Steve and Scot got out and Black immediately trotted across the street. He elected to climb the fire escape from below rather than finding a way onto it from inside the building. A.J. drove the vehicle away, leaving Blazer and Castillo on the street. Steve kept his eyes on the building, even though Loqueesha's windows actually looked out the other side.

In one minute, Steve's phone vibrated. Scot had texted: In position. In another minute, the phone vibrated again, when A.J. texted: No sign, I'm in alley. Steve glanced at the phone, then at Dave, and nodded across the street. They jogged across to the building.

Steve once again found the security gate unlatched. Someone inside really didn't care about security. They entered and climbed quietly up the steps. Steve led the way to the third floor and straight up to Loqueesha's door. They positioned themselves on either side, and first listened for any sound inside. There was too much noise from other apartments all around them to be able to discern anything from inside. Steve pulled out his phone and texted a warning to the other two: Ten seconds.

When time ran out, he knocked lightly on the

door. He waited several seconds to see if there would be any response. Finally, he recognized Loqueesha's voice shouting a confrontational, "Who is it?"

"Police! Open the door!"

He heard thumping inside, and the door was wrenched open. She appeared in the door. "Look, you pig—"

Steve saw in an instant that she had not repaired the chain from when they'd made entry the night before. He shouldered the door, shoving her back and pushing his way in, amid her protests.

"Hey!" she shouted, "You can't just—"

"Where is he?" Steve demanded. He made a show of drawing his sidearm from his shoulder holster. At low ready, he poked his head into her bedroom. The sun shined through partially open blinds, casting enough light to show the empty bed. He spotted a closet door and stayed to one side as he threw the door open and played his gun over the interior. He came back out into the main room, where Dave was standing in front of her. "Where is he?" Steve yelled again.

"He's not here!" she screamed.

Steve stepped up to her and Dave melted silently away to casually examine the apartment for any sign of Richards.

"Look, lady," Blazer said, his eyes staring her down. "He committed an armed robbery, shot at and physically attacked cops. We don't take that lightly. Tell me where he is."

"I don't know!" she screamed. She began to dance in place, shaking a fist up and down, and Steve saw her eyes giving up tears. She knew she was in trouble. "I don't know where he is. Just get the hell out of my house!"

Steve continued to stare her down, but he could see this was getting them nowhere. He gave Dave a quick nod to the door, and his partner walked that way. "We'll be back," he assured her, and left the apartment.

Steve quickly fished out his phone, and texted one word to the rest of the team: Rally. Moments later, as he and Dave exited the front door, Scot jogged up from the other side of the building. A.J. drove their unmarked Crown Vic up to Blazer's SUV as they gathered there.

"We'll head to his address of record next," Steve said. "But first, I want to stop by Green Resolve. Shaver should be shutting it down right about now."

* * *

In just minutes, they were once again stopping their cars at the tip of the Golden Gate Park panhandle. The scene was still flooded with police vehicles and the area was still roped off by crime scene tape. But Steve noted a handful of white Crown Victorias that had been pulled up to the crime scene tape and were blocking Baker Street completely. The DEA was here. He also noted that the crowds were a little different outside the tape. It was not the typical crowd of morbidly curious onlookers. As he politely excused himself through the crowd, he noticed how many were dressed. He was seeing a mix of the hobo-chic outfits of true addicts who didn't care about their appearance and thugs with sagging pants who just wanted their weed-high. As Steve ducked under the yellow tape, he began to hear jeers from the crowd. He looked at the dispensary as a DEA agent walked out, carrying a box. It would either be loaded with paper records or product.

Steve found Inspector Avery, and Shaver approached as he contacted him. "Where's our two employees?"

"I've got them stashed in one of our SUVs. Give them some leg room in the cage." He led Blazer and the DEA agent to a Police Ford Explorer parked in the intersection.

"Do you have their IDs?" Shaver asked the Homicide Inspector.

Avery handed over a folded three by five card. "I took their info from a Mexican ID card."

Shaver glanced at the names. "Yep, I've got them on my list."

Avery opened the door to the Ford Explorer. "Gentlemen, I'm Agent Shaver of the DEA. I have a warrant to search the premises for any evidence related to your activities with the Mexican mafia. I also have warrants for your arrest. According to the warrant, we'll be confiscating your records, computers, and any product that you have inside the shop." He handed the papers over to the suspects, who took them warily, like stretching gum from their fingertips. They started to look them over. "You keep those," Shaver said. He closed the door.

A strange cry and moan erupted from the crowd at the yellow tape as another box of evidence was carried out of the shop. It was taken to one of the unmarked federal vehicles and secured in the trunk.

Steve stopped to survey the growing crowds at the perimeter. He again took note that many of them were not the thugs that were the predominate customer he had seen during his previous surveillance. It was a mixed bag, some of the transients from the panhandle, several thug-types—and many of them appeared to be older, activist types.

Steve turned and walked toward the dispensary, entering the lobby.

Inside, the shop was crawling with feds in suits. A small stack of evidence boxes sat at one end of the counter. He saw that all products had been removed from the display cases. In a room behind the counter, he spotted two agents disassembling a desktop computer, a machine that seemed a little out of date. As he glanced around at the activity, he felt a small amount of satisfaction. A very small amount.

His eyes rested for a moment on the shattered glass at the other end of the counter. He suddenly turned and stalked back outside. He still had an armed robbery suspect to find.

His team fell into step with him. They marched past Shaver, who called after them, "Happy hunting."

As Blazer ducked under the yellow tape, he faced a few jeers from the activist crowd outside. Someone shouted, "We voted for this!" Another called out, "We're not going away!" Someone had the balls to actually shout, "The shit's legal now, pig!" He did not respond or react, except to shake his head. Hopefully Shaver was ready if they started to actively protest and impede his investigation.

"Officer," Steve heard as someone grabbed his left arm. He tensed briefly, until he saw it was a woman, short and grizzled. She was probably in her fifties but looked older. "I'm a patient here. What are you doing? How am I supposed to get my medicine?" Some of the crowd heard this and began jeering again.

Steve tried very hard to keep his face impassive. "Ma'am, this is San Francisco. There are dozens of pot shops in this city. I'm sure any of them will be happy to fill your needs." And with this, he felt his satisfaction melt away. He gently pulled his arm away and left her.

At their vehicles, Steve said to A.J., "I'll text you Lynell's home address. We'll meet there."

* * *

Kevin was getting sick of walking everywhere. Owning a bike in this city was nuts, too much work with all the hills. Sometimes he rode the bus, but that was for losers. Maybe he would look into ridesharing. There was no way he would ever get his hands on a car of his own. Especially now with his Dad dead.

When he ran from the scene of his dad's death this morning, he never stopped. He felt like he ran for miles, but after about ten minutes, he slowed down to a walk. As he gasped in breath after breath, he let the tears come. After all the shit he'd given his parents, it was his dad that seemed to want to pull him out of the mess he was making of his life. Kevin now realized that his dad was really the only one who really cared about him. Now he had no one. And no reason to care about anything anymore.

The tears didn't last.

He'd gone to school, but not gone in. The football team was still looking for him. Instead, he texted Randy Shepherd and begged him to ditch with him again. He waited in an alley just up the block from the school, a place where the "cool kids" often came to smoke before and after class, away from the school's "smoke free environment." He and Randy had become friends here at the beginning of the year when Randy introduced him to weed. When Randy heard that Kevin's dad smoked marijuana for pain from his work injury, he tried to get Kevin to steal some of his stash. Kevin always knew his dad smoked, but he never really tried to steal any. His dad had always been adamant that he steer away from this drug. But 'do as I say not as I do' didn't take, and Randy became his go-to guy. The more he tried pot, the more he liked it and wanted it. In Randy's world, the weed was plentiful.

Except today, for some reason.

Randy came walking up the street, glancing back toward the school to watch for any teacher demanding to know where he was going and threatening a call to the police. Kevin suddenly jumped out of the alley and grabbed him, pulling him in out of sight.

"Dude, what the hell's wrong with you?" Randy said quietly.

"I'm sorry, I just had to get away again. There is so much shit going on at home, you would not believe."

Randy could see that Kevin was distraught, more than usual. Parents were probably still riding him about school. "Your home life must be a total toxic waste dump."

"You have no idea. You got something I can take a hit on? I need to calm the brain cells."

"Sorry, bro, I'm barren."

Kevin suddenly leaned back against the backyard wall of someone's home. He covered his face, breathing into his hands. "I really have nowhere to go."

"Why don't we just go to Lynell's crib?" Randy asked. "In fact, I still have some pizza money my parents left me. Enough to get at least a couple of trees."

"Yes, thank you bro. Where does he live?"

The walk seemed to last forever. Randy babbled on about gossip at school. He did advise that the football team was harassing everyone they knew who was a stoner to tell them where Kevin was hiding. They were not letting go the assault on their fellow player. Kevin didn't ask, but Randy offered that Jessica Kline hadn't been in school the last couple days either. Kevin quietly wondered if she was with Lee, comforting him. Did he end up in a hospital? He didn't even know how badly he'd hurt the jock.

A thousand times during their trek, he wanted to tell Randy just what was going on in his life, that his dad had died just that morning. But he said nothing. He wasn't even sure he wanted to face it himself yet.

They cut across Golden Gate Park and into the Richmond District. Randy took him to 19th Avenue and up a block from the park. "This is the place," he announced. He approached a three-story building with businesses on the ground floor and apartments above. He approached the door to a Chinese laundry, but then pulled open the smaller door right next to it. Kevin followed Randy inside and up a flight of stairs. The stairs creaked loudly as they climbed. At the top, they made a U-turn and went down a hallway. One apartment door was on each side of the hall, and Randy knocked on one.

"Who dat?" someone shouted from inside.

"Lynell! Hey, it's Randy."

The door was wrenched open and Lynell Richards stabbed him with his eyes. He quickly leaned out into the hallway and checked for any other traffic. Only then did he confront Randy, "What the hell do you want?"

"What's up, dude? We're just looking for some trees. I got the bread."

Lynell regarded him with a stern eye for a moment, then nodded inside. The boys entered.

Richards seemed to be going through some chaos of his own, Donner observed. He had a couple of gym bags set up in his living room and he was packing clothes into one. Kevin, ever hungry for the marijuana high and now getting desperate, also took notice of some paraphernalia scattered around the apartment. On a table in front of the TV, he saw a large ziplock bag with several rolled joints. Lynell disappeared briefly into a bedroom, then reemerged. The light in the room was on, and Kevin could see a potted marijuana plant there.

"Look, kid, I got plans, and this is a really bad time. Tell me what you want so I can get us all out of here."

Randy handed over a couple of bills, and Richards pulled two small baggies out of one of his gym bags. Randy stuffed them into his backpack.

"Now, if y'all don't mind, I've got business, I'ma get the hell up outta here—"

Before he'd finished the sentence, the door to his crib was kicked open. Both Kevin and Randy jumped back at the impact on the door. Lynell made a move for his gun but hesitated when he saw who was at the door.

A well-dressed Mexican in a leather jacket stood there, playing a gun over the interior. He lowered his gun and took a step over the threshold. "Anyone mind if I come in?" he said.

CHAPTER 10

"Who the hell are you?" Lynell demanded.

"Are you kidding me, Richards?" the Mexican asked. "As many times as you've come into that shop, you don't think they recognized you? They knew when the cops unmasked your dead partner. I don't give a damn that you sell our weed to your own customers. But you can't just stick the place up. Everybody pays."

Randy was catching on to what was going on, and he didn't want any part of it. "Look guys, we're not part of this. You guys can work this out amongst yourselves, we'll just get out of your hair."

"You're not going anywhere, guys. You're going to stay right here." The Mexican adjusted his grip on his automatic, just for effect.

Kevin understood what was going on too. While the Mexican was distracted with Randy, Kevin slowly reached into his backpack.

"Hold it," he suddenly shouted, whipping out the revolver that Randy had loaned him.

The Mexican started, surprised that the kid had pulled a gun on him, but he made no move to relinquish his. Not to a scared little boy.

"I am having a really shitty day," Kevin shouted. "My dad died this morning, and all I want to do is smoke the weed I just bought. You guys can work out your own shit after we leave!"

Randy heard what his friend said about losing his dad and felt a heartbeat of remorse.

"Hell with all y'all," Lynell suddenly said. While the Mexican was distracted by Kevin, he pulled his own Smith and Wesson. "I ain't goin' out like dat."

The Mexican suddenly turned his gun back to Lynell. There erupted a moment of chaos, where everyone began to shout to put the guns down. The Mexican turned his gun between the kid and the black dealer. He shouted pleas for the kid to drop his gun, intending to plug Richards the second he did. But somewhere, he could see that the kid was too afraid to make this kind of choice, to pull the trigger. He turned his gun on Lynell and kept it there. The black dealer was shouting curses at all of them. He was still wavering between targets, shouting, cursing...

The Mexican had chosen his target. He suddenly fired. His bullet tore into Lynell's meaty torso. Richards fired as well. The Mexican tried to sidestep, but the bullet caught his shoulder. Both of them adjusted their aim and began rapid firing, and both riddled the other with bullets. They stumbled back, and finally collapsed at the same time. The Mexican died in the doorway. Lynell stumbled back, his fingers flexing and firing one more shot. He dropped to his knees and pitched forward.

His final bullet had struck Randy's temple, cored through his brain and killed him instantly.

Kevin had squeezed his eyes shut, but he still held the revolver up, now aimed at no one. When the silence enveloped him, he opened his eyes to see if he was dead.

The room was choked with smoke. He realized he was holding his breath, and let it out, inhaling that cordite. He began sucking in lungfuls of panicked breath as he beheld the carnage around him. The Mexican was leaking blood all over the entry. Lynell's blood was all over the wall. Kevin let out a soft cry when he saw Randy with half his skull gone.

With all the bloodshed, he realized that he had never fired a shot.

He choked off his cry and tried to get his breath under control. He stuffed the revolver back into his backpack. He had to get out of here. Lynell had sold Randy weed from one of the gym bags. He grabbed that bag and confirmed a pile of baggies and pill bottles with bud in them. He raised his eyebrows when he saw that a second gym bag was full of bundles and wads of cash. He also saw a large plastic bag sitting on a coffee table. It was full of rolled joints. He grabbed that bag and headed for the door. He stopped suddenly. Richards has a car, he realized, the Chrysler 300. He glanced around, searching for anything resembling a car key. He glanced at Lynell's body. He grimaced at checking a dead guy, but... he carefully approached, and felt the black man's pants pockets, careful to avoid any blood from his clothing. He found a bulge in a front pocket, and fished out a car key.

With his handful of bags, he bolted from the apartment.

* * *

Jessica Kline stepped out the main entrance of the Saint Francis Memorial Hospital onto Hyde Street. She turned to her friend, Elizabeth, who had come with her to visit her boyfriend, Lee. It was weird, there were other hospitals closer to their neighborhood, but Lee had been taken all the way to Nob Hill. He was suffering some pretty severe head trauma after getting beat up by Kevin at the party the other night.

"Thank you for coming with me, Liz," she said.

"No problem," Liz smiled sweetly.

"I just hope I did the right thing."

"Are you kidding? The police are going to nail that creep Kevin. He really messed Lee up, he may never play football again. He deserves some justice."

They glanced behind them as two uniformed police officers emerged. They walked up to the girls. "Thank you, Jessica, for talking to us. With your statement, we can talk to a judge and issue an arrest warrant for this Kevin."

Jessica only nodded.

"Can we give you girls a ride somewhere?"

Jessica smiled. "No thank you. We took the day off school. We were actually going to do some shopping. There's a Muni stop just down the block."

As the girls stepped away, Officer Pak commented to his partner, "Something about that name, Kevin Donner, it sounds familiar."

The girls approached the Muni stop. Elizabeth made a joke about a nearby man with a strange outfit on. The girls laughed, and for the moment, seriousness of their morning melted away. In moments, the girls were boarding an articulated bus, with the accordion-like connector in the middle and the electrical connectors on top. The bus pulled away, headed south toward Market Street.

As the girls found seats just behind the accordion-like connector, Jessica pulled out her cell phone and said, "I need to call my Dad."

* * *

Blazer slowed his SUV as he turned north on 19th Avenue. He searched the street for the familiar white Chrysler 300. He pulled to the side of the street when he spotted the vehicle just up the block. "Looks like he's home," he commented to Scot.

"What's this?" Scot suddenly asked. Steve had seen it too, a young white man running up the street. He reached the Chrysler and fiddled with the key, then got inside.

"Something's wrong," Steve said as he fished out his phone. When he reached A.J. in the Crown Vic behind them, he said, "You guys head up to the apartment. Something's weird, the blond kid just took off with Lynell's car."

"That's Kevin," Scot said. "We busted him and his buddy with Lynell the other day."

"Yeah, I recognize him." This is taking a turn for the strange, he thought. "I'm going to follow him."

When the 300 took off, so did he.

* * *

Kevin fumbled to fit the key into the ignition. The engine roared to life. He had his license but he rarely drove anywhere. His parents only had the one truck. Mom never used it; she took public transportation to get around, and his dad never let him drive the truck. At his house, getting his license earlier this year had been anticlimactic. Since then, he had only occasionally driven one of his friend's cars anywhere. When he hit the gas, the engine roared and the vehicle surged forward, taking him by surprise. He wrenched the wheel to pull out into traffic and wrenched it again when he felt his back tires screeching and the vehicle fishtail. He straightened out and headed up 19th.

He then reached into the Ziplock bag and pulled

out a joint. His hands were shaking as he held up a lighter and sucked pot smoke deep into his lungs. The act distracted him and he jerked the wheel again to keep the car from drifting too far into the oncoming lane.

* * *

As Blazer's black SUV continued up 19th Avenue after the Chrysler, A.J. pulled the unmarked up to the building. Steve had shown them which door led to the apartments upstairs, and they jogged to that door. Not knowing what they would find, they drew their weapons. A.J. pulled the door open, and Dave led the way upstairs. The creaking steps gave them away, but it couldn't be helped.

At the top of the stairs, he tuned and covered the hallway as A.J. passed him. The open door on the right was the first sign of a problem. A.J. positioned himself just outside. Rather than cross the open threshold and expose himself, Dave hugged the wall behind him.

"Police!" A.J. announced to anyone inside. He poked his head out to get a look inside, then suddenly pulled back. "I see bodies," he told his partner. Dave breathed a curse.

A.J. looked again. "One in the entry way. I see a back-bedroom door, light on, no movement. You cover the door; I'll track left and check the bedroom." Dave nodded. "Two, one," and A.J. stepped through the door. From everything he'd seen thus far, he wanted to establish a pathway through the apartment to at least clear it of threats so they could preserve any evidence later.

Dave stopped inside the door. A.J. moved behind a couch, his gun locked onto the bedroom door. He glanced briefly at the two other bodies bleeding onto the floor. He poked his gun into the bedroom and found no one here. "Clear," he announced.

A.J. holstered his weapon, but Dave kept his out for officer safety, covering the front door. A.J. took a moment to survey the bodies. "We have Lynell here," he said. He carefully felt a wrist for a pulse and found none.

"This is that Viejo guy Black identified from Green Resolve," Dave said of the guy inside the door.

"Jeez," A.J. said, "this is Kevin's friend, what's his name, Randy...Shepherd." With half his skull missing, Miano didn't even bother to check for a pulse.

"You smell that?" Dave asked. "Cordite smoke. This is fresh, happened maybe just minutes ago."

"Did Kevin do all this?" A.J. shook his head. "We need to stop this kid. Call and get a unit here to babysit this crime scene. I'll call Blazer."

* * *

Steve kept his distance from the Chrysler but kept it in sight. Kevin was driving erratically. He was all over the lane and weaving back and forth. He'd stopped at a couple of stop signs, and each time he started again, it was with a jerk and screech of tires.

Just blocks from the apartment, his phone beeped. Steve grabbed it and put it on speaker. "A.J., what's up?"

"Blazer, we got a bloodbath here. Three D.O.A. Lynell Richards is one. The second is Kevin's friend Randy. The third is Scot's Mexican friend from Green Resolve, the Sureño hit man. It looks like maybe these guys shot at each other and maybe Randy got caught in the middle, but...could Kevin have had something to do with it?"

"Jeez. Well, he is now a homicide suspect, until we find out more of what's going on. Get a uniform out there to sit on the crime scene until we can start the investigation."

"Already in the works."

"Call me back and I'll let you know where to catch up with us." Steve hung up his phone and handed it to Scot. He grabbed the microphone to the police radio mounted below his center console. "This is Wild Boy One, currently following a 187 suspect, north bound on 19th. Now turning east bound Geary. Requesting a marked patrol unit for a felony stop."

"Robert Twenty-four, I can be there in two minutes."

"Henry six, same traffic." From that unit, Steve recognized the voice of Suzy, his girlfriend, on the radio.

Steve's phone vibrated in Scot's hand. He glanced at the screen and showed Blazer.

"That's Shaver," Steve said, and Scot touched the screen, answering and putting the call on speaker. "What's up, Shaver?" Steve said loudly.

"Blazer, you won't believe this. We found some employee records and ran them for criminal history. We found a couple of parolees, which is a huge violation. We also managed to track down the real owner of the shop. He's claiming that these Sureños muscled in and took over the business right after he opened. They've kept him in the dark as to how things have been running. They just pay him off every week and he steers clear. Makes me wonder how many other shops are run by organized crime, or this specific gang."

"That it does," Steve said. "Listen, I'm a little busy, let me get back to you. By the way, our robbery suspect is now dead. I'll get with you for an update."

"Roger. Like I said, happy hunting." The call ended.

Just seconds later, the phone vibrated again. "Jeez," Black muttered at the heavy phone activity.

He glanced at the screen, and saw the number was restricted. Could it be someone from the department? He showed Blazer the screen. Steve shrugged. "Answer it."

He touched the screen. "Inspector Black."

"This is Officer Pak, we met the other day at that pot shop."

"Yeah, what's up?"

"You guys are looking for this kid, a Kevin Donner?"

Scot looked at Blazer and put the phone on speaker again. "Yeah, we're about to do a felony stop on him."

"Just to let you know his situation. We just took a statement from a girl at his high school. Her boyfriend is in the hospital, and she says Kevin beat him up pretty badly a few days ago. I checked this kid out some more. There was a 911 call to his address this morning. His dad had a heart attack and died right there on the front porch. We spoke by phone with his mom. She says he took off and hasn't been heard from since."

There was a moment of silence as they considered this new development. "OK, Pak, thanks for the info. We'll get in touch with you about that statement." He hung up.

"This just keeps getting better and better," Steve said. "This kid is going to be totally on edge." He grabbed his mike. "This is Wild Boy One. Units en route, be advised this suspect will be armed and very unpredictable. Officer safety, people. We're east bound on Geary...wait one." Kevin hit a green light and made a left turn, and Steve continued his broadcast. "North bound Divisadero. Suspect is driving a white Chrysler 300."

"Robert two-four, I'm making that turn as well, I should be right behind you." As he spoke, a patrol unit veered around his SUV and took the lead.

"Henry six, turning on Divisadero, I'm thirty seconds away."

A light ahead of them turned red. Maybe we just caught a break, Steve thought.

* * *

Kevin slowed at the red light. The joint sat comfortably between his fingers and he took a long final drag on it. He stubbed it out and immediately grabbed the next one, lighting it quickly. His hands were still shaking but getting better. It had taken a few minutes for the high to finally hit him, but now his nerves were tingling and antsy. His mind was racing through the THC. He didn't know what he was going to do, but he knew he couldn't stay here. Maybe he'd head north out of the city. There were lots of places in Humboldt and Mendocino Counties where they grew weed. Maybe he could hook up with some people there, start his own pot farm. In just a couple days, they wouldn't be able to harass him about anything to do with pot. Since he did not drive much, he had no idea where the nearest highway was. He'd need to look up Highway 101.

There were still a few other unresolved matters, such as the dead dealers he had left behind. But he hadn't shot anyone. What was the big deal? They couldn't do anything to him for that...

A siren chirped nearby, yanking him back to reality, jangling his already racing nerves. He glanced in his mirror. Through the tinted back window, he saw a police SUV, red lights on. The siren chirped a couple more times. He glanced forward. The light was green, maybe that's all they wanted. He hit the gas, maybe a little too hard, as the tires screeched briefly. The police car followed, lights still on.

"Shit, shit," Kevin muttered. He had a bag full of

weed and cash, and a gun. Considering all his interaction with the cops this week, he made a choice. He didn't want to get caught with any of this stuff.

He hit the gas.

* * *

The Chrysler suddenly sped through the intersection.

"Suspect is failing to yield," Twenty-four radioed. Steve heard his siren go from chirps to a full-on wail. Suzy's unit passed Blazer's SUV and her car lit up as well.

"This is Wild Boy One," Steve radioed, "I'll call the pursuit, you guys concentrate on the suspect vehicle. Currently crossing Sutter, suspect still failing to yield."

"He's speeding up," Scot said.

Steve concentrated on the pursuit. Ahead, Kevin fled from the lights and sirens. Despite the late afternoon hour, there was little traffic here. But there were enough cars for the Chrysler to duck and dodge between. "Suspect is getting reckless," Steve said. He was having his own hard time dodging around the vehicles, even though most were moving aside for the police pursuit.

"Coming up on Lombard and 101," Scot announced.

One block short of Highway 101, the light turned red. The Chrysler was still several seconds short, and traffic started. But he blew through the light. Several cars skidded to a stop, and one rear end accident occurred, a white Honda smashing into the back of a blue SUV. The police units one by one slid through the narrow gap left by the stopped traffic.

Ahead, Steve saw another hazard. Traffic was stopped at another light, two cars deep. Could they bottle him up there? Doing a felony stop there was risky with civilians in the line of fire. And once those cars left the scene, the suspect had a wide-open road again.

Kevin made another choice. Halfway through the block, he steered right—onto the sidewalk. The car bounced precariously and clipped a decorative tree, breaking it at the root. Steve cursed, seeing a group of pedestrians at the intersection. Through his closed windows, he could still hear the screaming as a dozen people scrambled to get out of the way of the charging car. People flooded into the street, causing east bound traffic to screech to a halt. This in turn gave Kevin a wide-open road. The Chrysler fishtailed briefly, then straightened out.

"East bound on Lombard," Steve radioed, "Speeds about fifty. This kid nearly ran down a group of pedestrians."

A new voice joined the radio conversation. "Aero-one joining the pursuit, over 101/Lombard."

"Good, helicopter overhead," Steve said, then radioed, "Welcome aboard, Aero-one."

Scot leaned forward, looking up and out the windshield. The police helicopter swooped overhead, about five hundred feet up. The pilot drifted across Lombard, then centered on the street and kept pace with the ground units.

"Robert-twenty-four, we have less traffic here," the lead unit radioed. "I'm going to try and position myself for a PIT."

"Ten-four, watch yourself," Steve answered. For the benefit of dispatch and others following the pursuit on the radio, he added, "Crossing Pierce."

The Pursuit Intervention Technique was risky, especially in an urban setting like this. It involved the officer maneuvering his car until the front bumper was aligned next to the rear end of the car so he could give it a shove and knock the vehicle into a spin to bring it to a stop. Steve had performed it many times.

The Chrysler veered into the number one lane, but then came across a pickup truck driving too slow and swerved back into the right lane. The lead unit closed the gap until he was nearly on the Chrysler's bumper. The Chrysler suddenly swung back into the fast lane. The unit would have been in a good position to now try the PIT, except for the slow-moving Honda that the Chrysler was dodging. The officer had to brake suddenly, and he changed lanes evasively, putting himself once again behind the Chrysler. They played the dodge'em game for several blocks.

At one point, Kevin in the Chrysler suddenly found himself boxed in by two vehicles, one ahead of him in lane number one, and another beside him in lane number two. Despite the police with sirens roaring, neither driver seemed to want to get out of the way. "Are they doing that on purpose?" Steve asked.

Kevin wasn't having it. The vehicles were still moving forward, so he swerved right, sideswiping the sedan next to him. He slammed his gas to the floor, rear-ending the car in front of him and knocking it partially out of the way. He then swerved right again, this time dragging the entire right side of the Chrysler against the sedan and pushing it out of his way. He gunned it again, accelerating through the intersection of Franklin and Lombard. The road climbed a gentle hill now toward Van Ness.

Traffic was stopped there as well. Kevin pulled the same maneuver he did before, hitting the sidewalk. People's attention was drawn to the police sirens, and they had at least some warning when the careening Chrysler sped up the sidewalk. They scattered into the street in front of the stopped cars. The Chrysler barreled into a stand of bushes in front of a hotel on the corner sending foliage everywhere. He steered right to head south down Van Ness. The rear of the 300 fishtailed and clipped a fire hydrant, breaking it off. Water instantly shot thirty feet into the air. A large pickup truck crossing the intersection, south bound on Van Ness, swerved to avoid being hit, and instead collided head-on with a smaller sedan in the north-bound lane.

"I'm calling it," Steve announced to his partner. "Aero-one, are you still overhead?"

"Affirm."

"This is Wild Boy One, I am terminating the pursuit. Let's let this kid calm down and Aero can track him."

Immediately, the sirens shut down. Both patrol units stopped behind the line of traffic and officers got out to assist those involved in the crash.

Steve leaned out his window. "Officer Wolf!"

She stopped at the passenger side of her unit as her partner ran toward the crashed vehicles.

"Get me through here! Use the sidewalk."

She glanced around, then motioned him forward. She ran ahead of his SUV, gesturing onlookers out of the way. Steve stopped short of the falling water. "Work this scene here," he called out to her. "I'm going to coordinate with Aero and stay with this kid." She nodded and ran toward the crash. He rolled up his window put on his windshield wipers and hit the gas.

The cops were no longer chasing this kid. But that didn't mean he didn't have to drive like a maniac anymore.

Steve sped down Van Ness, a major four lane road that dropped down a gradual hill. At the bottom of that hill was City Hall, the Civic Center. Steve saw that with traffic now stopped behind them, south bound traffic was not as bad. Kevin had a straight shot down the hill. Driving after him, Steve saw the

Chrysler picking up speed, bouncing as the road leveled out at each intersection, then gaining a bit of air and bouncing back to the street as it once again descended.

* * *

Kevin was jerked around the vehicle as it dropped from the sidewalk back into the street. He felt something hit the rear end with a loud thump. Whatever it was, he didn't care. He hit the gas and sped down the hill. He wasn't going to let the cops get him. He reached the level ground of the next intersection, then flew off that level ground when the road dropped away. His stomach soared up his throat, which felt weird with his high. The car landed with a crunch. He managed to keep the steering wheel straight. He dragged again on the joint dangling from his mouth.

A realization crept slowly into his brain. He couldn't hear the sirens anymore. He glanced around, jerking his head toward each window. Seconds later, when he again looked out the windshield, he had to swerve left to avoid rear-ending a stopped delivery truck. He fought to get the car back into control.

Nice piece of driving, he congratulated himself. He took a moment to check his windows again. Where the hell were the cops? They weren't chasing him anymore?

That didn't sound right. After everything he'd seen and done today, they had to still be after him, but there were no patrol cars behind him. Where were they? Did they have some secret way of tracking him? Hell, were they controlling his mind right now? Lulling him into a false state of confidence? Or were they closing in from somewhere he couldn't see? Any minute, this car could be torn apart in a hail of bullets. Any moment, some secret SFPD super cop was going to jump on his car roof, tear the damn thing off, reach in and grab his throat, and rip his head off. He'd have to be ready for that, ready for anything these pigs threw at him. He laughed at his new confidence. But then he choked off the laugh. These cops were serious. They had to be out there somewhere. There was some cross-traffic ahead, maybe he could hide there. He began checking his windows again.

He didn't see how fast he was approaching that traffic.

* * *

Speeding down the hills of Van Ness, Steve had a clear view of what transpired.

Kevin was dodging around slower vehicles, and Steve could see smoke occasionally puffing from his tires as they skidded on the pavement.

At the bottom of the hill, traffic was slowed crossing Van Ness at Grove Street, right next to City Hall. Kevin dodged around a slow-moving Buick, but then dodged back to the left, coming too close to a vehicle in the number two lane. He suddenly lost control. Steve was just two blocks away when he saw the articulated Muni-bus with the electrical hookup on top suddenly stop with traffic in the middle of the intersection. The tires of the Chrysler smoked as the wheels locked and the vehicle began to fishtail, but there was no stopping. The Chrysler smashed into the bus at the bellows, tearing the bus in half. The two halves parted, skidding aside as the Chrysler burrowed in and was suddenly lifted onto its side. People on the bus were tossed around, but a handful of unlucky people in the front seats of the back half were caught by flying car and debris.

***

In one of those seats, Jessica Kline was dazed following the crash. She opened her eyes to a sudden world of devastation. The side wall of the bus to her left was completely caved in and torn apart. She found herself slumped across the aisle of the bus. People behind her were panicking, and someone had wrenched open an emergency exit. Jessica checked herself, but saw only red. She examined the red and saw that her legs appeared twisted. One bone poked out of her thigh, and blood was flooding out from that wound. She began to panic herself, but another thought struck her. *If I'm hurt so bad, why can't I feel it?*

"Liz?" she managed to say. She looked to her left, where Liz had insisted on the window seat. Elizabeth's body appeared to be pinned to her seat by the collapsed side wall of the bus. Her face was free, but her lifeless eyes stared through her friend. "Liz?"

***

Steve sped through those last two blocks. He grabbed his radio again. "Major TC, right in front of City Hall. Suspect just took out a Muni bus. We need fire and ambulance, as many as possible. I'll run the scene for now, send some backup."

He reached the intersection. Scot had his door open and was running toward the bus. Steve was a half-second behind him, shouting, "I've got the suspect."

The Chrysler was on its side and somehow hooked on the bus. As they approached, it suddenly tore free and dropped, rolling onto its roof, wedged between the two halves.

As the car came to rest, Scot quickly checked for

dangers and saw that it was not on fire or leaking
fuel. He vaulted onto the undercarriage and took a
precious moment to steady his balance. He found
himself standing almost level with the floor of the
bus. He pulled on a piece of the sidewall and was
able to bend it away. He examined the interior. Most
passengers by this time had found their way off the
bus through the rear exit. But Scot found himself
face to face with two young girls. One was obviously dead, still pinned in her seat. The other's legs
were contorted to her right, and he saw a compound
fracture of her thigh. She looked at him with tears
in her eyes. "Help me!"

"Sit tight, sweetheart, help is on the way. I'm with
the police. You're going to be OK."

Meanwhile, Steve dove to the pavement and
crawled under the bus by the rear wheel of the front
half. The car shifted briefly next to him—that was
Scot jumping on above him. He edged away to avoid
being trapped. The Chrysler's windows were shattered, and he could feel the sharp corners of safety
glass fragments on the ground trying to tear into
the sleeves of his windbreaker.

He could see the form of Kevin inside, behind
the wheel. He pulled out his sidearm, and kept the
weapon trained on him, using his left arm to squirm
forward. By the front window, he rolled onto his left
side and played his gun over the interior. Being on
his side and looking at an upside-down suspect was
a bit of a mind warp for a moment. He saw no immediate threat. Everything loose inside the car had
now dropped to the ceiling. Steve saw that lots of
contraband had landed there, loose joints, pill bottles full of marijuana buds. Since this had probably
come from Lynell Richards' home, he knew some
of those would likely be from the recent robberies.
A backpack sat upside down against the smashed

windshield. He saw the barrel of a gun sticking out the top. Steve reached in and grabbed it, dragging it carefully out. He stuffed it under his tactical vest.

Kevin suddenly opened his eyes and saw the cop in the dim light four feet away. He did not give any immediate indication that he recognized Blazer from the previous bust. "Hey!" he shouted, "Hey! Get me out of here!"

Steve shook his head. "Sit tight, kid, help is on the way." He stared Kevin down for a moment, then said, "Happy New Year, kid. Was it worth it?"

Steve holstered his gun and squirmed out from under the bus, emerging from the eerie dark and quiet to the blazing chaos outside. He jumped onto the overturned Chrysler. He checked the front half of the bus, which was also now empty. "What do you got?" he asked of Scot.

Black had found an abandoned jacket on a nearby seat. "Hold pressure here," he said to the girl. He briefly turned to Blazer, and said quietly, "One DOA next to her. This one has a compound fracture and possible spine injury."

Steve leaned in to the girl. "Miss, what's your name?"

She struggled to say, "Jessica."

"Jessica, you're going to be fine, but I need you to do one thing for me. Whatever you do, I need you to try not to move too much."

"Is it my back?" She suddenly asked, tears streaming down her check. "I can't feel my legs. Am I paralyzed?"

"We don't know, kiddo, but I want you to remain as still as possible. My partner is going to help you keep pressure on that bleeding. We've got paramedics coming, they'll be here any second." As he said this, sirens in the background suddenly became louder.

Steve jumped off the overturned car. An ambulance was just pulling up, and he ran to meet paramedics. As they got out and eyed the details of the crash, Steve announced, "We have one teenage female inside, possible spine injury and bleeding from a compound leg fracture." The medics nodded, and with a new sense of urgency, they hurried to the rear of their rig for the gurney.

When the medics reached the back of the over-turned Chrysler, Scot announced to them, "She's in and out of consciousness from loss of blood."

One bold paramedic grabbed an X-collar, a neck brace, from a bag under their gurney and he jumped onto the vehicle undercarriage. "Let me in there."

Scot backed out of the way, and the medic went to work. He reached down and pulled the second medic aboard. Scot jumped off.

He found Steve conversing with the first fire truck crew on scene. "One injured, possible spinal injury. Her friend is dead right next to her. Our suspect is still trapped inside the car underneath, but can we make sure the girl is taken care of first?"

"I hear ya, Sarge, we'll do what we need to do."

Steve backed off for the moment, allowing the other emergency crews to go into the wreckage and do what they did. He did keep a special eye on the Chrysler, making sure Kevin did not make it out and somehow escape. He kept reflecting on his words to the kid, at the end of his drug addled run from the law, and from the consequences of his actions. But the words had a dark double meaning, reflecting on how helpless Steve's fight against drugs in general sometimes felt.

Was it worth it?

EPILOGUE

The marijuana issue had come right to the front door of City Hall.

Steve and Scot were joined by the rest of the team. They had to coordinate the processing of the scene of the triple murder. A.J. had taken some digital pictures of the apartment before the uniforms arrived to guard the scene and he showed them too to Steve, walking him through what he believed had occurred there. Lynell and the Mexican had apparently shot each other and Randy was simply caught in the middle. From the cursory photographic evidence, Steve had to agree. The gun he took from Kevin would be checked for ballistics; in case he had contributed to the shooting. Each collision he had caused along the route of the pursuit would be another crime scene for him to coordinate the processing of and another charge against the pot-head. Steve spent much of the next hour on his phone, coordinating CSI and Homicide teams to each location and processing what they told him of their findings.

Kevin was the last 'victim' to be pulled from the wreckage. Jessica's ambulance left long before that. Fire crews had to use the "jaws of life" to further tear apart the bus, and a tow truck to winch the back half of the bus away so they could pull him out. Scot oversaw his extraction and noted that he was awake and complaining of leg and back pain. He made sure the crews knew that Kevin was in custody and he picked a random uniform to babysit the suspect en route to the hospital. He finally returned to where Steve was just finishing a phone call.

"The tragic irony," Scot began, "is that his injuries would give him a perfect excuse to smoke medicinal pot."

"Too bad, they don't have pot in prison," Steve muttered.

"Blazer, you're naïve if you think that's true."

Steve smirked. "You're right." His smile drifted away as he took in the fire crews working on the destroyed vehicles, the police officers circulating among the other passengers, taking statements. The dead girl was covered with a sheet provided by the fire department and they were now preparing to extract her.

"This is why I do it," Steve said quietly. "This is why I fight the drug war so passionately. It's not about personal use, it's not about what one puts into their own body. It always affects someone else. I try to protect that person."

"I hear ya," Scot agreed.

"Blazer!" someone else shouted. Steve couldn't believe he was hearing the voice. He turned to find ADA Kline marching up to him. "You did this?"

"What are you doing here, Kline?"

Kline skipped the question. "You were pursuing a suspect that did that? My daughter was on that bus! She may have spinal injuries!"

Steve anger melted away. "Oh, man, your daughter is Jessica. Have you heard if she's going to be OK?"

"You were engaged in a vehicle pursuit? Is that

what I heard? When a pursuit starts to endanger the lives of innocent people, you're supposed to terminate and back off."

"I did," Steve said.

Kline went on like Steve had not even spoken. "You're supposed to back off and pick the guy up later when he's not so hopped up. Now this druggie that you've pursued has crashed and killed someone and almost killed my daughter."

"I'm sorry about your daughter, Kline, I truly am. But there's more to this. This kid is not just some random pot-head. He was involved in a triple murder. He ran from the scene. And yes, when this pursuit got too hairy, I terminated it. The records will show that. Unfortunately, this kid did not get that message, and he kept running."

"And now he's killed an innocent girl. You're responsible for that!"

Steve remained silent for a moment. It was pointless to plead his case now; it was pointless to run the distraught ADA through the events that led to this kid Kevin being at the site of a triple murder where his friend was killed. It was pointless to tell him that Kevin was panicking, that his life had spiraled way beyond his control, and he was riding high, smoking stolen marijuana, joint after joint, when he ran from the cops.

"Tell me again, counselor," he finally said. "This pot-head is some innocent kid caught up in police business? Tell me again that marijuana never killed anyone."

Kline threw up his hands and tried to walk away, but Steve was not done with the pushy DA. "Tell me again, Kline!" he shouted, following him. "Tell me again that this shit doesn't kill! Tell me again!"

A LOOK AT BOOK FOUR:
BLAZER: SHOT IN THE DARK

BLAZER WANTS THE TRUTH, EVEN IF IT MEANS RISKING HIS LIFE.

In the 1990s, SFPD's Special Forces was shut down under mysterious circumstances. Now, the city faces a criminal crisis, and the once-forgotten unit is reinstated with Sergeant Steve Blazer in command. But Blazer inherits more than just a new squad. Special Forces has a legacy of corruption, and he aims to create a new reputation—one full of trust and determination.

As a shocking high-profile murder rocks the city, evidence points to murder/suicide committed by an Assistant DA. But the more Blazer investigates, the more leads turn into dead ends. Meanwhile, a prominent political figure has Special Forces assigned to his security detail and soon after has an assassin on his tail. As Blazer digs, he discovers that not only is this political figure a former Special Forces cop, but he also once commanded the squad. Who is trying to kill him? How does it connect to Blazer's other case?

Blazer makes an agonizing deduction: his killer is a cop. He sets a trap to bring the culprit to justice. But if he takes down a corrupt cop, will the department approve of busting someone who tarnishes their image? Or will the brotherhood of cops turn its back on him forever?

COMING FEBRUARY 2022

ABOUT THE AUTHOR

G.C. Harmon became interested in action heroes at a very young age: cops, firefighters, soldiers, even racecar drivers and cowboys. At the age of 10, he discovered writing, and began by creating short stories based on his favorite TV characters. Around the same time, he created the Steve Blazer character, and has been developing the character never since. As a teen, he discovered the pulp fiction genre, authors writing books with the kind of heroes and stories he aspired to write himself, favorites including the Executioner and Destroyer series. Fresh out of high school and seeking more knowledge on what he was writing about, he joined the Military.

Over the next fifteen years, G.C. Harmon spent time in the United States Army and Army Reserve, first with Artillery as a Forward Observer, then with the Signal Corps. He capped off his military career with a tour of the Middle East in support of Operation Iraqi Freedom. He trained as a cop, graduating from California's Peace Officer Standards and Training Police Academy in 2000. He has worked in the Security industry since 2002, working alongside many police departments.

G.C. Harmon has had many crazy life experiences, some of which find their way into his stories. In 2017, after exploring mainstream publishing and finding no opportunities, he took the plunge and self-published his first Blazer novel, "Red, White and Blue." Through self-publishing, he made new contacts in the publishing business and discovered Wolfpack Publishing, putting out the kind of exciting adventure writing he has done his entire life. He lives in Sacramento, California, and he is always working on new Blazer adventures.

CPSIA information can be obtained
at www.ICGtesting.com
Printed in the USA
LVHW100922100122
707900LV00005B/108

9 781685 490058